ROBERT MORAN
PRIVATE

ROBERT MORAN

PRIVATE

KEN CATRAN

Lothian
BOOKS

Dedicated to my father and to Bentley Catran

The author gratefully acknowledges a grant from Creative New Zealand which assisted in the preparation of this book.

Thomas C. Lothian Pty Ltd
132 Albert Road, South Melbourne, Victoria 3205
www.lothian.com.au

National Library of Australia
Cataloguing-in-Publication data:

Catran, Ken.
Robert Moran: private.

For young adults.
ISBN 0 7344 0688 6.

1. World War, 1939–1945 — Campaigns — Africa — Fiction.
2. Korean War, 1950–1953 — Fiction.
I. Title. (Series : Lothian YA fiction).

NZ823.2

Cover illustration by Declan Lee
Cover design by Michelle Mackintosh
Text illustrations by Gaston Vanzet
Text design by Paulene Meyer
Printed in Australia by Griffin Press

THE MORAN QUARTET

Robert Moran — Private is the second book in the Moran Quartet about a family whose war spills over into peace.

In *Jacko Moran — Sniper*, we begin the story. Jacko is a slum kid whose street-wise smarts make him a good soldier and a deadly sniper. He wins the Victoria Cross but, at war's end, has no place in a peacetime world. The demons of wartime trauma follow him always. His son Robbie swears never to be like him.

But the Second World War comes and Robert joins up. He has the same skills as his father — and is driven by the echo of violence. War engulfs him as it once engulfed Jacko. Robert has sworn never to forgive his father, but violence and bloodshed bring a strange redemption.

The forthcoming third and fourth books will continue the saga of Jacko's family.

Jimmy Moran — Regular: Jimmy Moran is a regular soldier like his father. But the ghost of old Jacko lingers and the family will divide over Vietnam.

Teresa Moran — Singer: Teresa is the daughter of Jimmy. She wants to live up to her father and fights to gain acceptance among her male comrades, realising at the same time how the resonance of war has destroyed her family. In Iraq and Timor, she is put to the test. Can she break the cycle of wartime and peacetime violence that has always beset her family — and find the courage to change the future?

Korea, 1950

IT IS COLD. Everywhere is frozen and white. Even when a flare goes up, red into the black sky, its colour is lost in the ice. I am frozen too, because even layers of clothing bring no warmth in this wasteland. I am busting for a leak but won't; even our urine is a weapon of war here.

Sound carries a long way in this stillness. I can hear a very distant crump-thud, just above my own heartbeat. So the Marines are still copping it at Chosin. Beside me, my loader rearranges the bloody machine-gun belts for the umpteenth bloody time and spits on the frost-rimed sandbags. He has a cold — we all do — and his mucus sticks from his nose like icicles.

There is only silence and icy darkness before us. But they are out there somewhere and they are coming. And this time — maybe — we will not stop them.

I should be home. I should be shooting rabbits for the bounty. Slinger's got three second-hand car yards now — 'emporiums' he calls them — and Harris is running for Parliament with sod's own chance of getting in. I suppose Ernshaw'd be running a bank, but he's in one of those big ceme- teries outside Cairo.

So what am I doing in Korea? Waiting for the Chinese Fourth Army to come over that hill. I'm scared, so maybe I should think about Mirella. That will make me angry and I can take it out on them. Or maybe they will take it out on me.

'Tough buggers,' breathes Shank beside me. His breath puffs in a white cloud over the neat ammunition belt.

He's thinking of the Fourth Army. All of us are, dug along this ridge. Tough, yes, dedicated and bloody good at what they do. Even though we are wrapped up in winter gear and they have cotton uniforms and rope-soled shoes — oh yes, and they are conscript peasants, malnourished on a handful of rice a day.

Clip-clop, clip-clop, went our shoes on the linoleum floor. The hospital dark, smelling of carbolic and disinfectant. People snoring in the wards as we passed. We turn into one of those wards, a woman in a spotless white uniform waiting.

'Father Pat, I don't want this, I don't want to see him.' But I don't say this aloud, and his firm hand on my elbow pulls me along with him. Clip-clop, clip-clop go our feet down the line of beds. Now I can hear another sound.

'We'll stack them up, eh, Robbie?' hisses Shank. More of his white-clouded breath drifts over the thick barrel of my gun.

Yeah, you said that for the umpteenth time, Shank, trying to convince yourself, mate. Because they may just stack us up, because sometimes there is no stopping them. Deluded, low-intelligence; obsolete weapons, says our US Liaison, a gum-chewing South Carolina red-neck.

Wake up, mate! These 'conscript peasants' are the Chinese Communist Army who fought the Japs to a standstill with their 'obsolete' weapons. Who then cleaned up the Nationalist Chinese Army and took over all China. Who have

8

now come over the Yangtse river to help their North Korean comrades clean up South Korea. Who have already knocked the crap out of South Korean and American divisions. Who have surrounded America's best troops — the Marines — at Chosin Peninsula. Deluded, low-intelligence? Yeah, so how come the Marines are in the deepest of shit? Air-power and artillery have not stopped the 'deluded peasants' at all.

Maybe because they are not deluded, but bloody good soldiers; bloody good at what they do. And all on that handful of rice.

Mirella.

Using her death to make me angry? Then why the hell am I here!

Now. What made Korea 'now' for me? How did I get here? North Italy, Mirella's scrubby little village; then, after the war. Before all that was North Africa — and before that … oh hell, joining the army. Before that, 1940 and the bloody clean-smelling hospital. Father Pat —

The hospital and that ward, clip-clop, clip-clop — that other sound I could hear.

It's like a harsh rattle, the nurse in her white starched uniform leads us towards it. The end bed has a yellow light overhead; a man lies there, still, the white sheets tucked under his chin. Now the harsh breathing rattles like a train in a tunnel.

Oh hell! He rolls an eye towards me, red-faced, blubbery and wheezing, the saliva spittle on his stubble-rimmed lips. Now he chokes, a flood of yellow phlegm that the white-starched nurse wipes away. A word coming out of that croaking plug-hole sound.

'Faith — faith!'

Reading something in my eyes, turning that bristly red face away. His breath like the low croaking of a rusty engine, then stopping — the white-starched nurse blocks my view. Father Pat's hand tugs me away. 'It's over, Robbie.'

So I squeeze my eyes shut, knowing that in this pure frozen wasteland will come shrill discordant bugles in the black frozen air. Then they will come, elite uniforms outlined against the white snow. They will come in their outflung lines, each overlapping the next, another after that, never ending —

'He's gone, Robbie, and now y're the man of the house, and'll look after your mum, I know that.'

Father Pat and I are on the steps of Wellington Hospital and red dawn has given way to cool morning air and the rattle of passing trams. My father is dead and it means nothing. Father Pat's warm handshake means more.

'Ye're the man of the house —' So does that mean I can crush lead soldiers and pass out on the floor with a pillow under my head? Be like him —?

This man of the house is damn near frozen solid. Soon our artillery will open up. Then our mortars. Then it's machine-guns and automatic rifles and just working a damned bolt. And those white-outlined snowmen will fall and die and keep coming. They will be blown apart, stitched all ways with bullets, and leave a bright frozen red on the snow.

They will keep coming because there are so bloody many of them and they are very good at what they do.

And when they come, we may die. Because we must hold this ridge with our lives. Just as they must take it with their lives.

Let the bullets and pain freeze like the night. Let me scrunch my elbows into the icy mud and puff my own frozen breath.

Geeze, Father Pat — man of the house — easy for you to say!

Too damn cold to think, think about warm, think about North Africa and sunlight shimmering hot, and black flies —

Why the hell did Father Pat haul me there? Hadn't seen the old boy for years, didn't want to see him die —

What the hell? What the bloody hell? All that was years ago and will not change the path of one bullet now. I may die soon but it does not matter. I'd rather think of Teresa or Creel — that awful sodding mess!

'Cripes, Robbie, I'm busting,' mutters Shank.

'Tie a knot in it.'

Because I'm busting too, but the temperature is below zero. Our damn guns will freeze and the only source of warm salty liquid available is our bladders.

Clip-clop, clip-clop, I didn't want to see him —

Like a wailing sound of unmusical death, come those bugles. They break the black morning air, giving full intent of their purpose. Time to fight and time to kill. Time for battle and let the tears freeze on my eyelids. Because memory and hate and simple bloody anger churn together as I squeeze the trigger —

Come on then — time to die!

And the loud jarring clatter of the guns fills my ears, dinning out my angry thoughts — because they are coming and I am good with this gun, short bursts, sweeping it back and forth. As they come and come and fill the sights with their white bulking mass.

I shoot and I kill and if the gun freezes, I will pee on it. And I will be full of screaming anger behind my tight lips and slitted eyes. Not at them. At me, at the bloody hospital and bloody Africa, at the bloody army I joined to escape my bloody father. Bloody Italy and Monte Bello, hell, Mirella and bloody —

The bloody loud noise of this, bloody thunderous; my finger tight on the trigger. The loud incessant noise is good because it drowns out thought —

I didn't want to see the old bugger!

New Zealand, 1940

SO I WAS on the steps of Wellington Hospital. So it was a cool wartime morning. Already there were warnings in the papers about sugar and even pork chops. All of it kept for the 'lads'.

I was one of the lads. Not that I saw much sugar or any pork chops. Not that I'd figured out why I had joined the army. Of course we had screw-all airforce or navy. And, anyway, I would have been conscripted.

Oh, it was okay to get photographed, get the headlines: JACKO MORAN'S BOY, and SON OF VC WINNER JOINS UP. And never mind that I was seventeen and under-age. The new and clumsy hand of government propaganda did not care. I was Volunteer of the Month. Even photos of me and Mum were staged. Didn't anyone see that, from her wooden face and scared look?

So it's 1940. So my father served in the last war and even won a Victoria Cross. So he was a sniper in no-man's land, so he was a hero when the German Army nearly broke through. No. None of those reasons. I joined the army to escape, and I was depending on using Old Jacko's reputation to get me a 'cushy number'.

The New Zealand army was pretty small then. Growing fast, but still using all kinds of outdated crap.

Even the food tasted like it was left over from the last war. They even tried to make a tank out of a tractor and corrugated-iron. Yes, believe it. They did have some weapons that weren't outdated or rusty, or falling apart. These were also left over from the First World War and were called 'non-coms', which means non-commissioned officers.

Sergeant Seaton was one of them. He was short and nearly bald, with a big jaw and gleaming eyes. He looked like someone had poured him out of a mould, khaki uniform and all. Like he was issued out of a stores manual.

Anyway, about my third day in the army, he grabbed me. 'Private Moran, do you know who I am?'

'Ah, Sergeant Seaton, sir.'

'Do not 'sir' me, my lad. I am not an officer. I am a non-com and I work for a living. Geddit?'

'Ah, yes, sir — I mean, sergeant.'

'I have been watching, Moran.'

'Sergeant?'

'You are coasting, my lad. You think you are entitled to some kind of special number here, don't you?'

'No, sergeant.' Yes, actually, but no way was I saying that.

'Oh yes, you do, my lad. Hero's son and all that carry on. Oh no, Moran. I think you have what it takes to be a soldier and I am going to make you one.'

'Sergeant?'

'I do not care if your dad was a war hero. I do not care if your dad was King of Siam. Or if he was best mates

14

with Mr Hitler, Mr Churchill and Mr Stalin. All I care about is turning you into a soldier. Geddit?'

'Yes, sergeant.'

'No, you don't, my son. You don't get it at all. But you will — and never mind being Jacko Moran's boy. You will wish you had never been born. Geddit?'

'Sergeant.'

'No, you don't, my son. But you will.'

He gave me a horrible ferocious grin. It was about the only time I saw him smile.

OH, YES — and my dad's funeral. Big military turnout, even a general. A lot of talk about his finest hour in the trenches. Nothing about after the war, the drink, the work camps and jail time. He was dead, therefore a hero.

Me, red-faced, in a new khaki uniform that itched like hell, wondering whether to salute or shake hands. A too-tight glossy leather belt. Jumping a little as the volley was fired.

Mum in a new black dress — don't know who coughed up the dough for that; Aunt Francesca probably — holding her rosary, a couple of nuns with her. Black veil over her face, even a tear or two. I didn't have any. Even a decent coffin with a brass nameplate. Robert Thomas Moran; I was named after him. Mum throws a little earth, I chuck a full handful and make sure it lands on that brass nameplate.

Goodbye, you drunken abusive bastard — good riddance. I have no tears!

A fancy reception too, and who laid out for that?

The general, red-faced with a white moustache, talks about our pantheon of heroes, whatever that is. Then a Colonel Fields, who talks about Jacko being a 'casualty of peace'. Gets a look from the general.

Last, a politician, plump and pink-faced. Assoc. Minister of Something, leans on a cane. Also fought with Dad (who didn't?), name of Creel. Says Jacko was cast in the stamp of the true Kiwi fighting-man.

And when he belted Mum for her last bob and hocked her rings for drink? When he belted me for looking at him sideways? Smashed my sister's doll through the window? Passing out on the sofa, gone the next morning and away for months; the other kids chanting, 'Jailbird Jacko.'

I get overnight leave from the barracks, spend it with Mum and Sis, Uncle Joseph too. He says, Jacko's paid for everything now. *He never paid for anything, you stupid* — I want to shout. Mum doesn't mention Jacko at all. Why should she? He was just about never there.

So in the morning, I'm back to the army — and Sergeant Seaton.

AT FIRST, ALL the blokes in my barracks are just strange faces to me. Most have heard of Jacko Moran, the VC winner. So I get a few looks, like I'm special. Rumour is that Jacko's boy pulled strings. That he's up himself.

The barracks are two rows of plain hard beds and rough army blankets; windows open at night. It toughens us up. So does the food — at least it doesn't kill us.

I do keep to myself. One or two try to make me open

up, the others just leave me alone. The officers do treat me like I'm like special, but that stops too. I get to know the other blokes though. Listen to them talking.

Needham, Harry. Otherwise known as Slinger. A skinny ferret who sold second-hand cars, wants to get into the Quartermaster's Office. To keep him out of the firing line, he's quite open about it. 'Slinger' because he's always slinging it out.

Bates, Gerald F. is disgusted at this. Helps run a scout troop and says this war is about our way of life. Chaps like Slinger don't set a good example to his lads, and would we mind not calling a chap 'Gerry', because it sounds too German. He'll answer to Batesy.

Harris, Ian C. just hoots. He's a Red (and proud of it) and this is a capitalist war, that's why communist Russia is staying out of it. It's about bankers and merchants getting rich on the blood of the working man. Yes, he's said this before and — hey, the next bloke who throws a boot at him gets one back.

Ernshaw, Malcolm R. is a ledger cadet at the post office with fifteen quid saved and the war means he'll lose promotion. He's got nothing personal against Germans or their Mr Hitler. And, listen, a chap's entitled to his opinion without being called rude names.

Mulligan, Neville. Farmer. Worried because most of the shearers have joined up and old Kemp's the only one left, and he always takes too much off, so Lord help the sheep if there's a cold snap. Nobody gives Mulligan a hard time, because he's built like a brick bungalow.

Tilly, shop assistant, Rayner, a truck driver. Bristow,

Conway, Breen, three Smiths and two Browns — a few weeks ago, all civvy lads getting on with life. But now Hitler's Panzers are running amok in France and Belgium and the French are caving in. And the whole Brit Army's penned in a town called Dunkirk, no chance of getting away. And Harris says the war will be over in three months — six months tops.

Crazy to find I'm thinking about Jacko. But he knew barracks, men like these and army routine. I'm about his age, too, but don't feel close.

I wish I could stop thinking about him. Getting trained by Sergeant Seaton helped.

Square-bashing, equipment and rifle-training, inspections — yes, and route marches. Tramp, tramp, tramp went our boots and bark, bark, bark went the sergeant.

'Straighten up, Moran, hitch your pack up and step lively. This is a route march, not a shuffle round the ballroom floor. And keep your gob shut, otherwise you will swallow dust. Then you will drink, then you will get a stomach-ache and be even less bloody use than you are now!'

Rifle-training and inspections.

'Moran! My old Grannie holds her brolly more like a soldier than you hold that firearm. And if I hear you call it a gun once more, then you will peel potatoes till your fingers fall off. It is not a gun, Moran, what is it?'

'A rifle, sergeant.'

'No, Moran! It is a .303 Lee Enfield, magazine-fed

and bolt-action rifle, and just about the finest bloody firearm in the world. Look after this rifle and it will look after you! Now present it to me for inspection.'

'Sergeant.'

'Now, when you present this firearm — smarten up, you slovenly soldier! — you open the breech and stick your thumb in, so that when I look down the barrel, I will know that it is not loaded. Otherwise it might blow my bloody head off and then I would be seriously annoyed with you, my lad.'

'Sergeant.'

'Do you call that clean?' I have seen rifles twenty years on the bottom of the harbour looking better than that. You are peeling bloody spuds, my lad, what are you doing?'

'Peeling spuds, sergeant.'

'Correct. What are the rest of you smiling about? What are you smirking about, Ernshaw? I am going to inspect all your rifles and if you spend this war peeling spuds or cleaning latrines, then someone has to do it. And why not the most horrible unwashed bunch of misfits ever landed upon a sergeant? Who should have joined the German Army — because that is the only way you will ever help us win the war!'

'Moran, what particular exercise are we engaged upon today?'

'We are stripping and reassembling a Bren-gun, sergeant.'

'A thirty-round, magazine-fed, automatic rifle to be correct, Moran, but I will overlook that because of this. What am I holding in my hand, Moran?'

'Ah —'

'A screw, my son. More properly, a screw that belongs in the automatic rifle you have just reassembled, which would then break down in the middle of action. And if I was firing this Bren, Moran, I would end up with a German bayonet in my guts and then I would be very seriously annoyed with you, my son.'

'I'm peeling spuds again, aren't I, sarge?'

'You read my mind, Moran.'

'Moran, what are we engaged upon?'

'Target practice, sarge.'

'Yes, my son. And you have put eight shots out of ten in the bullseye. That is better than every other so-called marksman in the platoon, so does that make you a better shot, my son?'

'Suppose it does, sergeant.'

'You suppose it does, do you? Well, son, when a Hun stormtrooper is coming at you with a sharp steel bayonet on the end of his Mauser, then you might know different. Then it will be too late for you to know the difference, so what do you do, my son?'

'Practise, sergeant?'

'Yes, son. Geddit?'

So I do practise. Because old Jacko handled a gun well and I want to be better. I want to break down a Lee

Enfield and — blindfold — assemble it. Also, blindfolded, break down and assemble a Bren gun.

And fire same in practice. Stay longer than the others and shoot till the light goes, never mind if I miss meals. My eye red from squinting down the barrel, my shoulder like a horse kicked it, from the thud of the butt.

I will do it better than he did!

Yes, and still scowl. Yes, and let Sergeant Seaton know he cannot push me around. Yes, and learning the most basic army rule — that he is a sergeant and I am a private.

'Moran! Do you know what the army has a never-ending supply of? An abundance what never stops?'

'No, sergeant.'

'Potatoes, my son. Spuds, Murphys, Brown Boys, whatever they are called. Now since I have just inspected your locker my son, do you want to guess where this pleasant conversation is headed?'

'Me peeling spuds, sergeant?'

'You peeling spuds, my son.'

I'm peeling spuds again. These are big knobbly brown ones, full of black spots — slow and boring work, and Sergeant Seaton has promised stacks more if I don't get them all done 'double-quick'. It occurs to me that old Jacko may have peeled potatoes in this same place. Maybe on this very stool — it's old and battered enough.

A shadow in the doorway and I stop. A man is there, in civvy clothes, a nice pinstripe suit and overcoat draped around shoulders. He removes his hat. Greying brown hair, a thin, lined face. 'Private Moran?'

Not another bloody reporter. And if I get one more 'going to win a VC like your Dad', he'll get a bucket of spuds over him. He takes his coat awkwardly from his shoulders with his left hand. He has no right arm, just about no shoulder too. The sleeve's tucked neatly in the jacket pocket.

'Captain Rowlands, late Wellington Battalion.' He sits down, touches the empty sleeve with his hand. 'Late nearly everything at Amiens. I was there with your dad.'

Amiens? Oh yes, the last big German push. Sergeant Moran rallied B Company and they fought to the last man.

'I was his company captain in Flanders.'

I drop a half-peeled spud back into the bucket. Here we go, another old-timer who served with Dad, oh brave as a lion he was — lot to live up to, son. I'm braced for this and suddenly aware Rowlands has a shrewd smile. He laughs.

'You want to tell me to rack off. He would. The same sod-you look. Insubordinate, uncouth, foulmouthed — and the best natural fighter I ever served with.'

'So how come he never made general, then?'

'I said fighter, not soldier. He'd sit on the trench and blaze away at the Huns like he was bullet-proof. And no more deadly sniper — ever tell you about his duel with Dead Willi?'

'No.' I'm listening though, somehow sense Rowlands isn't like the others.

'Took out two machine-gun nests when our attack failed, once. Saved all our hides.' He chuckles. 'Even so, he only got the VC because some Pom staff officer didn't know Jacko was being rude to him.'

'I hardly knew him.'

Rowlands nods. 'We lost touch after the war. He was all over the place, work camps, on the road or —' He stops. I think 'jail' would have been the next word.

'He was a bastard.'

'He was a fighting bastard. Nobody needed his skills after the war. A land fit for heroes, eh? Men in uniform were spat at.'

Rowlands owns about six department stores now. Seems genuinely sorry he couldn't help Dad. He tells me more in half an hour than I ever knew. Even about the fabled Mannlicher rifle Jacko took from Dead Willi — knocked into scrap in a last battle.

Rowlands looks at his watch, tightens his lips like he's thinking hard. 'Robert, Jacko's own dad was a drunken layabout. He had one hell of a slum childhood. War was the only thing he did well. Don't hate him, son — hate's no good. You might end up like him.'

End up like him? What the hell does that mean? Rowlands gets up, stiffly hooks his coat back around his shoulders. I hold out my hand, he takes it. As though the action reminds him, he takes something from his pocket.

'You might like this.'

'This …' is an old brass-shelled rifle bullet. Some curly lines are deeply scratched down one side. He presses it into my hand.

'Jacko's,' he says. 'Taken from a Turk sniper at Gallipoli. Jacko carried it through the war, his lucky bullet. The scratched writing on the side is a Turkish word — faith.'

Rowlands somehow kept it when Jacko was wounded. 'I'd been meaning to give it back to him.'

'Thanks, Mr Rowlands —' I nearly say 'Captain'.

'Robert, war's tough. It can go on breaking you, even when it's over. It broke Jacko — nearly broke me. I'll keep an eye on your mum. And look me up when it's over.'

He means this. I sense it's the promise he was never able to keep with Dad.

'All right, Mr Rowlands.'

He makes to go, another pause, his lips tight now. 'Your dad never mentioned our company major. One Rupert Creel?'

Creel. The name rings a faint bell, the bloke at the funeral? I headshake. 'Never mentioned him.'

'Then I won't. Good luck, Robert.'

And he's gone. I sit thinking, then pull up the bucket of spuds again. My drunken dad did have the respect of some soldiers. And Creel — a hint of secrets. Then a voice like a wood-rasp at the door. Sergeant Seaton.

'Moran! You will finish those spuds in one hour — even if you spend all night doing it. Geddit?'

'Goddit, sergeant.'

I pick up the knife, cut my thumb and curse. The bloody army, my bloody father. I make one promise to myself — to stay a private.

Barracks again. Another bloody long route-march today, lights-out soon. I'm getting to know the others by listening to them talk — the ones who do all the talking. Tilly's quiet like me, just listens and smiles.

MULLIGAN: You gotta admit it's a bloody miracle. The Poms pulling three hundred thousand men off Dunkirk like that.

HARRIS: Miracle? It was a balls-up. Hitler's kicked their arses back to Pommyland and that's no miracle, son, that's bloody defeat. Uncle Joe was right to stay out of this.

MULLIGAN: Uncle! You related to Joe Stalin or something?

SLINGER: Think of it, lads. All those French towns, Dunkirk itself up for grabs. I bet the pickings were good.

HARRIS: Uncle Joe has told world communism to stay out of this war. My conscription is against my political beliefs.

ERNSHAW: Why don't you write to the Prime Minister about it? Hey, watch your language, Harris, that was a sensible suggestion.

SLINGER: Think of it. Jewellers' shops, rich homes, department stores. I heard some blokes did a bank, got away with gold bars. Bet the bloody officers took it off them.

MULLIGAN: What d'you reckon the Poms'll do now?

ERNSHAW: President Roosevelt has pledged to keep them supplied.

HARRIS: Aye, Yanks'll do anything for a buck. And we're next. Cannon-fodder to save the bloody Empire. Churchill and all those grouse-shooting chinless wonders don't give a stuff about us.

SLINGER: A nice spot of gold bullion. That'd do me.

ERNSHAW: My friend Charles in the company office is making up shipboard regulations. We may be going soon.

MULLIGAN: Sooner the better.

Most of the blokes were writing letters. I'd written once to Mum, been to see her on leave. We hardly say a damned word to each other. She wants a photo of me in uniform. Harris is off again about Uncle Joe, and I go outside. Up comes the crunch of outsize boots.

'Reveille soon, Moran. Get your head down.' Sergeant Seaton coughs and thumps his chest. 'Don't know what they're using for tobacco these days.'

'We shipping out soon, sarge?'

'Maybe. Never thought I'd say this, Moran, but you're coming on all right. Now get in there and tell that bolshie bugger if he doesn't stop shouting the odds about Joe Stalin, I'll do it with the toe of my boot.'

'Yes, sergeant.'

'Moran.'

'Yes, sergeant?'

'We'll be on the move soon. Very soon. Get your letters writ and see that mum of yours. Geddit?'

'Yes, sarge.'

'It's a shower, son, it's a bloody shower. We did this twenty-odd years ago and now we're having to do it again. Nothing bloody changes. Just do your job, son and keep your head down. Best advice I can give you.'

I go back inside. Only later I realise just how good his advice was. Worth more than medals and being a damn hero. And like all good advice, I'll learn it the hard way.

So we're shipping out. Word is Britain, for the invasion of Europe.

Greece and Crete, 1941

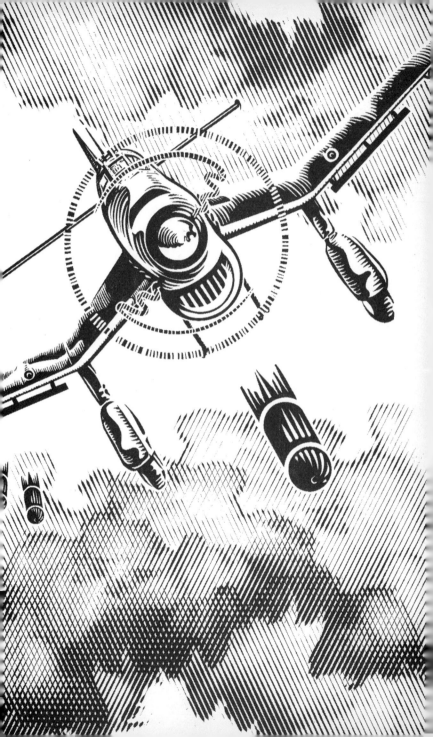

Greece, 1941

Bob Conway unscrews the cap and the radiator boils over. He mops his face with the same oil-stained rag and looks around. A long 100-yard hike to the river for water, and he curses. 'Fair bloody cow for heat, this place.'

Off he goes. Conway is right. Greece, in summer, is a fair bloody cow for heat. We are on one of those narrow dirt roads, full of dust. Our platoon on 'mobile reconnaissance' until the radiator boils over.

Slinger shifts the rifle off his shoulder and rubs a hand there. He squints up into the blue sky — very blue and a very golden sun overhead. The sweat streams off his face as he does. 'Why do those bloody birds keep circling over us?'

'They're kites or buzzards,' says Ernshaw, who actually takes an interest in these things. 'Carrion-eaters —' Even Ernshaw, though gormless, is not clueless and breaks off.

Mulligan (who is still thinking about the sheep-farm) jumps right in. 'Carrion — you mean dead meat?' And breaks off too. Our section is in the shelter of a stone wall. No cement, just dry stones atop each other and they clatter when we shift against them. We are tired, dirty, hungry and thirsty — and bad-tempered. An eight-mile hike under the Greek sun will do that. More so when you're packing sixty pounds of battle-gear.

Dead meat? Plenty of that waiting ahead like the distant rumble of gunfire. Maybe we'll be dead meat soon, because there's a German armoured division up there — rumour is they've cleaned up the Greeks — just like the Greeks cleaned up the Italians. Rumour is we get cleaned up next.

'I'm dry as a bone,' says Bristow, our radio man.

Slinger tilts his helmet over his eyes. 'Couple of blokes in B Company got some wine. Want a pack of fags per bottle,' he mutters, still looking up at those circling birds.

'We shouldn't be here,' says Harris. 'This Greek Premier, Mega-whatsisname, is practically fascist himself. Thieves falling out, that's what this is all about.'

'Write to Uncle Joe,' muttered Mulligan.

He gets a laugh. Actually this fight is about Hitler's mate, Mussolini, deciding Greece is a nice easy target. So his crack Italian divisions come over the mountains and get booted back — twice. So the Brits move in, with us and the Aussies.

So did Hitler, bailing out his fascist mate.

'Keep a sharp lookout for aircraft,' shouts our Lieutenant Challis, skinny and knock-kneed, with big spectacles. It was Challis who pointed out that my dad fought at Gallipoli, across the waters. Yeah, so what, Mr Challis?

Sergeant Seaton is ahead. He's picked up a tummy-bug, sweating and pale, but still a damned good soldier. Looks back. 'Slinger, Ernshaw, get up ahead.'

They do get up — quickly. Slinger will give anyone an argument — except Sergeant Seaton.

They clump on ahead. There's a little rise ahead, by a burned cottage. The villagers long fled — we passed them on the road. Women in black, old men pushing barrows, kids carrying wicker cages full of hens. Kids tearful, snot-nosed, bare-footed on the sharp stony roads. They pass without looking at us.

I look up at the black bird-spots circling overhead.

So I will be fighting soon. That ties a knot in my stomach because I am scared. Scared of not stacking up to my mates. Yes, and resentful; I bet old Jacko never knotted up his guts — just got on with it, pig-ignorant brute that he was.

I have the Bren, Tilly the spare clips. He passes me his water bottle and I take one swallow. You don't let a mate run short. The river water's okay for radiators, but not for us.

'Reckon we'll find the Jerries soon?' he asks.

Yes. Or they'll find us on this sun-baked road, shimmering with heat waves like a burning river.

Those overhead birds. Something funny about them, these new birds flying in a straight line. I tingle, feel a prickly joy of warning. It is mad, unpleasant, but thrills like icy-cold delight. Battle-warning, battle-danger. I jump up.

'Listen!'

Four black spots flying in a straight line and they are not birds. And in the stillness, there's a lazy and almost silent sound like the drone of faraway bees.

'Aircraft, take cover!' shouts Seaton. 'Tilly, Moran, get your Bren fixed on the wall.'

And even as he shouts, the birds are no longer birds, but straight-winged aircraft dropping out of the blue skies. And that lazy silent sound becomes an ugly snarling drone. And those ugly straight-winged aircraft tilt towards us. They are German bombers and they want to kill us.

So Sergeant Seaton and Lieutenant Challis are yelling. I listen to Seaton, mount the Bren; its tripod scrapes on the stone wall. Remember gunnery lessons, aim ten yards in front — and my hands are trembling because — *oh shit* — this is war, this is being killed, this is Tilly babbling in my ear —

'Not yet, Robbie, out of range, not yet —'

'Shut up, Tilly!'

I know about guns, I know about range, hell, I know about babbling too. I am locked to the Bren; I know this gun and it will obey me. *Shut up, Tilly!*

Now the big straight-winged aircraft — Dorniers, someone shouts — are falling from the blue sky towards us and their snarl is deafening. Everyone's taken cover, Challis jumps into a tumbledown pigsty. The engine-roar thunders towards us.

We fire towards it. It thunders louder. Now the black closing specks are large two-engine bombers. I squeeze the trigger, a full thirty bullets gone in no time, click-click. Tilly jams on another magazine, screaming, 'Get them, Robbie!'

On a thirty-clip? I squeeze the trigger, but those down-screaming bombers just keep coming. Tilly clicks on another clip, the black lines of tracer streak upward. A whistling loud scream now, louder, louder —

'Duck!' screams Tilly.

I hit the ground as the drystone wall scatters. A large chunk bounces off my steel helmet. Solid blinding dust and chunks of debris slam down; the Bren is blown away somewhere and I'm rolled over, winded, spitting dirt as the smoke clears.

The loud ugly droning is fading to that lazy-bee sound. Up in the blue sky, now smoke-thinned, the aircraft angle steeply over those grey-brown hills and the sharp dazzle of sunlight. A hand grabs me.

'Robbie, you okay?'

Tilly. I nod, spit out more dirt. I think one tooth is broken. My cheek's smeared warm and sticky from a cut under the eye. Tilly is nursing a bruised hand, looks up to where the German aircraft are just black bird-specks again.

Five minutes — less?

We stand. Black smoke rolls from our shattered truck — all the spare food and ammo was on board. A crater where Slater and his radio were; what's left of them both is splattered everywhere. Nearby, Harris and Bates get shakily to their feet.

Sergeant Seaton stays on the ground. Most of his head is missing, bright red blood all around him. Bright as the yellow sun and blue sky, I think confusedly. It doesn't register that Seaton is dead — it doesn't seem possible.

Watkins comes running up, jacket torn, his tin helmet askew and dented. He tips it back level. 'Bates, you're acting-sergeant, Tilly, acting-corporal. Salvage what you can, get a grave detail.'

Tilly gives me that job, grins at my look. Four men hastily buried, six wounded. Putting Seaton's body in doesn't seem real — hell, he was chewing me out yesterday. McGregor's nearly dead, every bone in his body broken by flying stone. He begins to scream, a high screeching animal sound — gets shot full of morphine. Won't last an hour.

One body we can't bury. The stores lorry is well ablaze and Bob Conway, once apprentice plumber, is behind the wheel. He's carbonised black now, his body contracting, one arm pointing straight up as though accusing his attackers.

Fair bloody cow for heat, this place!

Death, bloody and violent, has slammed us all. But I'm working, checking the Bren — like there's a detachment, pushing the horror away. Did my old man think like this — and why think of him?

We're pulling back.

WE'RE IN A little village, still on the plains. The war seems to have stopped for a day or two. We get a new lieutenant to replace Challis, who has fallen ill. Short and slim, pink-cheeked and fair-haired. Neat uniform, glossy leather and gleaming brass. One out of the band-box.

And the first thing he does — sends for me!

He's got a room in the mayor's house. Furniture smashed, door and window fittings gone for firewood. Everything Greek, people and animals long gone.

'Private Moran!'

'Sir.'

'I'm Lieutenant Creel. Richard Creel.'

An odd look as he says this, like he's expecting me to react. I don't and he purses his lips, speaks again. 'Obviously the name means nothing to you.'

'Sir?'

'My father is the Hon. Rupert Creel — spoke at your father's funeral. Major in the battalion — in Flanders?' Again that odd catch and little look. Like he wants a reaction? Yes, I remember that old boy learning on a cane, but that's all.

'Didn't know a lot about my father, sir.'

Creel just nods. A pause. His gear's half unpacked on a lopsided table. There's a thick black leather-bound book with gold lettering. I crane my head slightly to see it. 'Ili—'

'*Iliad*,' says Creel. 'Know it?'

'Some kind of medicine book, sir?'

'Not that kind of illness.' His face is very smooth, hiding a smile. 'Epic poem, Greek classics — you know?'

He's been posted here in London. Finishing a degree in England when the war broke out. Speaks Greek — ancient Greek — so they posted him here. And he wants me in his platoon — as lance-corporal.

'Don't want to be Lance-Jack, sir.'

I get a very direct look from those pale blue eyes. 'No? Well I'd rather be finishing my thesis in Cambridge. But I'm stuck with this and so are you.'

'I don't want promotion, sir.'

There are flies buzzing and a goat bleats in the distance. It had better not let Slinger hear it.

'Your father made sergeant.'

'Sod my —'

I break off. But realise I have told Creel as much as he wants to know about me. He's a shrewd bird, will bear watching. Now he nods, that odd look again. 'All right. Just be my top marksman. Achilles with a Bren, eh?'

He smiles. I don't know who Achilles was but smile back — you do when officers joke. And he's letting me do the one thing I'm good at — using a gun. I salute and go.

Outside, I register something. Without meaning to, I've told young Creel a lot. And he's got me on the same job Jacko was good at. Does that crafty bugger think he's placed me?

He hasn't. I tell myself that. *He hasn't.*

The goat has stopped bleating. Slinger is nowhere to be seen.

We fall back. Regroup. Army terms that I pick up on quickly because they mean retreat. Because we were chucked into Greece without enough men or equipment to make a difference. Because Jerry has the pressure on. His divisions are well-equipped and his tanks are bloody good. Our anti-tank guns? We might as well piss.

And he has command of the skies. Which means we get to know German aircraft really well because every day Dorniers and Heinkels and Junkers bomb us to hell then bomb us again.

Stukas are the worst.

Lieutenant Creel is shaping up. Always last on his

feet, getting us what supplies he can. Using his Greek on the villagers for food and water. Shouting encouragement and even bawling verses from his bloody *Iliad*.

'I think that bugger's enjoying this war,' mutters Slinger, and he's not far wrong.

'He's a good officer,' says Bates, who's made up to sergeant. And of course, writes to his scout troop with the good news. And to Evelyn, his 'intended'. She's in the guides, a sort of female Bates.

Bates corners me one night. Dinner was a handful of black olives and a chunk of sharp-tasting white goat-cheese. Slinger had some cans of bully (army beef) but I couldn't afford his prices.

'Moran,' he says. 'There are questions being asked about you.'

Me? Questions? I'm on sentry-go and there's a half-bottle of wine that I shoved out of sight when Bates came up. Bates takes his duties very seriously indeed. There's a serious look on his face now.

'What sort of questions, sarge?'

'I have to be honest, Moran. You're the son of a war hero and you show no interest in promotion. No interest at all.'

Bates is a heavy-set guy, square-faced and looking very solemn. He's sitting, hands clasped in front of him, and staring intently. I'm one of his scouts up on a charge. Wrong answers and I'll lose my woggle or lanyard. I've had these lectures, though. I know how to handle Bates. First an outraged look, mouth open and eyes wide.

'Geeze, sarge, thought I did a good job!'

'Well, you do, but —'

'Swear I put bullets in that last Heinkel.'

'Sure, Moran, but —'

'Right after sentry-go, I'm talking to Lieutenant Creel. I want to know who's spreading this crap about me.'

'Oh, cripes, Robbie, nobody's doing that. I mean your Lance-Jack stripes are there waiting.'

I look wooden, set my mouth and stare ahead. 'I'm not the man my dad was, sarge. It has to come when I'm ready.'

'Sure, Robbie, just thought I'd have a word,' and Bates stands up hastily, clattering rocks. 'You let me know.'

And off he goes. Yes, I'll let you know, Bates, some-time never. That white cheese is sharp in my mouth but a swig of wine will — I discover the wine-bottle is over-turned and the contents out.

So I'll do my last sentry hour with my throat like sandpaper. Cursing Bates, cursing his sense of duty, the scouts and even Evelyn. Scouts — hell, I lasted one week as a wolf cub.

Finally my dad is doing something useful — helping me avoid any damned rank.

Bren gun

WE HAVE LOST this part of the war. Even the officers have stopped using 'regroup' and 'fall-back', because Jerry has us on the run. Our company, our battalion, just included among a shambling column of weary, dirty men. We pass hasty graves and burned-out wrecks. Rifles, helmets, canteens, blankets, flung down.

'Ditch that thing,' mutters Slinger. I'm still carrying the Bren, Tilly the spare clips. Slinger has already 'lost' his rifle. 'We're moving too fast for Jerry to catch up.'

Wrong move, Slinger. Creel comes up, sees he has no gun. No excuses. Slinger ends up humping two rifles, not that he'll get the message.

One time we do turn and fight. There's a bridge ahead, jammed with vehicles. So we — the rearguard — take our places to wait for the Germans. For once, there are no aircraft overhead; of course, they have their pick of targets.

'I hear the Brit Navy's waiting to take us off,' mutters Tilly, beside me.

The Brit Navy? Bloody good targets they'll make for the Junkers, Dorniers, Heinkels & Co. I am dog-tired, fighting sleep and ready to drop.

Did you feel this, Dad?

Old Jacko's still intruding so I shut him out. There's about a hundred of us in this action, command by Colonel Douglas, ex-lawyer and bloody good. He's laid us in every little fold of ground overlooking the road. Tilly lays the spare clips, clinking.

My Bren is a damned good weapon. They cost the

Army about fifty quid each, about my pay-whack for six months. Smooth, easy to handle, easier to jam, but I like my gun. Lying behind it, squinting down the sights, I feel a great sense of — yes, belonging. Doing something I am good at.

Aunt Francesca: '*Young Robbie won't amount to much.*'

Uncle Joseph: '*Plenty of jobs the lad can go into. Post office —*'

Well, sod you both, I am here in Greece, the sun is bloody hot and I am behind a fifty-quid gun, so I can do something —

Ahead, Creel is using his binoculars. A flap to us, keep down. In the distance, a spindly wee Jerry aircraft, 'Storch' they call them, is sussing out our troops. It swoops over the bottle-neck ahead and wheels away.

Careless. But they know we are on the run.

Too bloody careless.

First, a couple of scout-bikes come into view. Gunners in their sidecars. They stop only once to look through binoculars. Little black figures on their little black bikes.

They get closer.

Behind them come trucks, one a covered Bedford. They're picking up our equipment as they go. They stop, troops get out, pulling equipment after them.

Slinger is one side of me, about to light up a fag. I slap it away before Bates can. No warning. Ahead, the Jerries are setting up mortars, they'll drop their shells right on the bridge. Sunlight flashes on binoculars as an officer takes a look. Creel bellies up, points to the German mortars.

'Fix on them, Moran.'

The Germans are quick but assured, trained troops, and I have no feelings about them. I don't need Creel muttering about getting back at them. They are there and they will die.

Did Jacko feel like this? His lucky bullet's in my pocket — hell, he did his first fighting not far from here. The sweat trickled into his face. He watched the enemy, squinting down the sights, finger on the trigger. Were they easy like these are, shirt-sleeves and forage caps? They are going to die.

Hell, they would do the same to us!

There is no 'open fire' order. A machine-gun starts over to the left, there's scattered rifle-fire and the whistle of our own mortars. My German mortar team are springing into action as I press the trigger.

Tac-tac-tac. Short bursts. Tac-tac-tac.

The loader is slipping the bomb down the mortar-tube. The bomb fires but it's the last. He jerks back. His mate tossed aside, I shift to another man who jack-knifes down.

I'm not feeling a damn thing, Dad! Was it this easy for you?

Three dead, I still target.

It's over, in stuttering murdering minutes. Jerry's a little too careless and the survivors run. A couple, too brave, setting up a machine-gun. Tac-tac-tac, my bullets sparking off their gun as they are thrown back.

I am detached, cold; they are dead, I shift target.

And it's over. Short and bloody. A last truck lurches

as the wheel goes, the windscreen shatters. The driver escapes because I'm slapping a clip on. Otherwise I would press the trigger and watch them die — and feel not a thing.

Killing is so damn easy. A hell of a habit that I slip into easily. There's a popping in my ears, my elbows scrunch on the sharp stones.

'Well done,' says Creel.

And we have orders to fall back because Jerry will be back in force. With their damned Heinkels and Junkers, Dorniers and — of course — the Stukas.

There's time for a quick run over. Creel wants the enemy equipment destroyed, shouting that we're cast from the mould of Ajax and Hector, whatever that means.

He grabs a map-case from a dead officer. Slinger, whooping with delight, gets the gold cigarette-case and binoculars. Me, I walk up to the men I personally killed.

That unreal prickle, like when Sergeant Seaton died. That detachment like the real person in me is just looking at this. Like this is not real — *Seaton's head blown away!*

There are three men hit by my bullets. The loader's shot through the neck and face, his spectacles smashed. The second is taller with black short hair and bristly stubble around his mouth. Not standing too close to the razor — hell, I peeled potatoes for that. The third is doubled up and still breathing, hands over his shot guts and blood spreading, his eyes rolling up whitely to me. Fair-haired, pale under his sun-tan, blood on his lips and dying. Even with my brief experience, I know that.

Who are you? Did you have a father like Jacko? Did you think it would end like this, looking up at me! I am offering you a cigarette, but you are locked in a private horrible world of pain.

Slinger's beside me, with a Luger pistol and two watches. He winks, pulls another watch from the dying man — dead, his eyes rolled up blank and white. His rattling breath stops on his blue lips. His arm flops as Slinger pulls the watch off his wrist.

Creel yells for us to regroup and we head back to the bridge. The bottleneck cleared, we get across as the engineers lay their charges. The bridge blows, crashing into the gully, the steel girders wrenched apart.

Creel is beside me. 'It'll take Jerry maybe half a day to throw another bridge across,' he says wearily.

A hundred miles to the sea. So we set off again, looking up at the blue sky. That is where the sudden storming death comes from, gull-winged and screaming like lost souls.

Stukas.

Breda machine gun

WE ARE ON the slopes of a mountain called Olympus. Across the plains, smoke rises from the bombed villages. Each is a shattered milestone to mark the Panzer advance.

There's a distant noise too — 'cump, cump' like a giant's slow advancing footsteps.

But this is a quiet day, under shady olive trees, away from the blue and yellow blazing heat. The Germans are leaving us alone, but Acting-Sergeant Bates is not. Give some blokes a stripe and they're bloody Hitler.

Creel says Mount Olympus is the home of the ancient Greek gods and perhaps they will join us against these modern barbarians. That's fine with me; let them deal with the Panzers and the Stukas. Sooner them than us.

We are filthy and dead-tired, our ragged uniforms stink and we are half-starved. By a miracle, mail has caught up with us. No food and little ammo, but mail. Good to read and useful to light fires with. Acting-Sergeant Bates keeps his, says they are going into his scout troop's archives one day.

Slinger laughs. A bill for some car-parts he bought; the bloke has less chance of getting payment from Slinger than I do of lining up Hitler in my Bren sights. Slinger reseals, writes 'RETURN TO SENDER' over it.

Ernshaw sighs. The Post Office Savings Bank has overpaid him by one shilling and nine pence. This will be deducted against his wages (upon return to civilian life) and he is requested to be more careful in the future. Ernshaw is worried that this will affect his grading. So will a German bullet, says Harris.

Tilly curses. Mum sent him a jar of her marmalade and some crook rat at HQ must have nicked it. Slinger collected the mail today and I wondered why he was licking his fingers so much.

No mail for me. Mum doesn't write a lot — well, at home, we never talked a lot. Mulligan's got a letter from his wife, she's had a son. He gets some 'well dones', a laugh or two. But he's frowning, looks at me.

'Hey, Robbie, what do you know about being pregnant?'

I groan. The sun is hot and I want to sleep. 'Nothing. I promised Mum I wouldn't get pregnant and I'm keeping my word.'

'Come on, Robbie, you know what I mean. Women.'

'I think Robbie promised his mum about them, too,' says Slinger.

Okay, I don't chase women like some of the blokes. But Lieutenant Creel is near and I don't want my officers getting the wrong ideas. If Slinger's hinting … he's not, from the hasty way he looks aside.

Mulligan has both hands out, waggling each finger as he counts. 'Robbie, does nine months count from the er — from when it's a baby?' he bites his lip. 'And is the month it's born an extra, sort of making it ten months?'

Mulligant wants those ten months for ease of mind. I don't know what to say but Richard Creel cuts in — just before Ernshaw, who is smirking.

'Babies are like trams, Mulligan. Always late, never come when expected.'

'Thanks, sir,' says Mulligan, with relief.

Ernshaw has a smart comment on his lips but I accidentally kick him as I stretch out. It's too hot for a fight and home is a distant, different world away.

Tilly nudges me. 'Hey, Robbie, got another letter.

I'm accepted in Agriculture College. When I get back, of course.'

Sure, Reg, now shut up, I want to get some sleep.

'Cattle-feeds, that's the future. Lucerne, chou mollier; cripes, something that grows like ragwort —'

I must have accidentally kicked him, like I kicked Ernshaw. Home, letters — dreams. I will trade all that for the blue sky staying free of gull-winged screaming dive-bombers, for a few minutes' sleep and no Stukas.

Stukas. They are a bastard. German fighter-bomber, single-engine, two-man crew. 'Gull-winged' they are called, but show me the seagull with those bent wings. Obsolete, say our officers, sitting ducks for our Hurricanes or Spitfires; sure, if our own fighters are around. If not, then the Stukas are screaming black murder out of the blue Greek skies.

So we are getting near the coast; on one of those narrow stony roads made for goats not soldiers. And ahead, through the hills and shimmering heat, is a glimpse of blue water. Lieutenant Creel, bright as bloody ever, yells, 'There it is, the wine-dark Aegean.'

If he doesn't stop spouting this classical crap, some-body is going to shoot him. Probably me.

Our trucks grind in low gear, a croaky noise that rolls up the column. The flies hit our sweating, dirty faces, hover on our cracked lips. Grind, go those gears, clank-clatter, rattles our gear; an ambulance goes past, with the moans of wounded men. All the dull quiet sounds of defeat.

Yes, and Reg Tilly. Okay, we're mates but no more about ragwort or blackberry; or the crop estimates of alfalfa and barley. And listen, Moran, do you know what Professor McElrea said —

'Shut up!'

I'm not yelling at Tilly. I'm picking up on something like I'm tuned; looking up at the blue sky and those tiny black dots in the far distance. Like tiny black flies, except they are forming into line and dropping towards us.

'Aircraft!' yells Creel. 'Ernshaw, ha, the Lewis. Tilly, Moran, the Bren.'

We are all diving for cover. Brakes screech as the trucks stop and the drivers jump out. I heft the Bren on its tripod, cursing — 303 bullets! May as well piss on them —

'Remember, fire ahead!' yells Creel.

Good advice, lieutenant, like we never heard it before? These dots already larger and silhouetted into gull wings. Dropping, dropping, and from the blue silence comes that unforgettable sound. The scream of a diving Stuka.

You have to hear it to understand. It's the sound of everything you hate — from something under the wings — like nails down a blackboard, like a grindstone or a dentist's drill. Getting steeper and louder till it dins through every-thing. Like harsh, cruel hate.

'Fire!' yells Creel.

The loud jabber of the Lewis gun, of my Bren. Thump-thump-thump against my shoulder, the brass shells popping out. The first Stuka overhead, wing-gun twinkling, the black bomb released, adding its own shrill whistle to that evil piercing sound. The bomb explodes behind us. Tilly is jamming another clip onto the Bren.

'Bloody awful noise,' he grunts, with a scared grin.

Sure he's scared, so am I. No time to think, the second Stuka is screaming down now, the second black bomb whistling, and this explodes closer. Rocks and dirt fly, ahead a man is tossed over and over. Beside me, Tilly's hand slips on the clip.

'Tilly —' I yell, because the third Stuka is falling.

He just slumps, his eyes shut like he's sleeping. And there's a little hole, very small and black-edged, just above one eyebrow. No blood, but when I grab his shoulder, his body rolls.

No, he is not dead, he cannot be dead because Tilly is my mate and it cannot happen like that. And me grabbing the clip, snapping it onto the Bren, knowing he is dead — feeling an anger that's sudden as the shock of death.

The third Stuka is screaming down.

'Keep down!' yells Creel.

He yells that because I am standing. But his voice is just a tinny squeaking. And this rage makes me stand, gearing me up like a mix of hot and cold fire. Bringing up the Bren to my shoulder, I'm a big lad; I'm good with this gun, Sergeant Seaton says. And it's like everything slows down, even the Stuka-scream does not matter.

Firing. Tac-tac-tac-tac and I'm so keyed up, I'm seeing a neat pattern of minute holes appear on the yellow-spotted snout behind that red propeller. The black bomb whistling, I am shoved suddenly down, the bomb explodes behind.

Creel has pushed me — saving my life. Even so, that anger is still clicking, I'm grabbing for another clip. He shoves me hard.

'Stay down —' he breaks off. 'Holy old Zeus, you got him!'

The first two Stukas are back high in the blue sky. The third below and wobbling, the gull-wings shaking, Creel yelling, 'Achilles split his head at the brow with hilted sword — fine shooting!'

Not fine. I lower the Bren because suddenly it's too heavy. And I should be putting on a fresh clip. Tilly should be handing that to me. Tilly who is huddled to one side. Oh, get up, mate, I know you're asleep. Mulligan's turning him gently over, looking up at me.

'He's had it, mate.'

So what about ragwort, Tilly, alfalfa, lucerne, what about that stuff? Geeze, you can't just finish like that. It's not fair!

It's just not bloody fair.

So Reg Tilly is dead, so we sort ourselves out. Tilly's body in one of the trucks, Mulligan takes over as my loader. The drivers start up, squinting nervously into the blue sky. The Stukas have gone, the smoke has faded.

Some of the blokes look at me, Moran, who fearlessly stood up and clobbered the Stukas. Well, they know sod-all; it was stupid anger that nearly got me killed. I think Creel knows that — I get a shrewd enough look. Then he's waving his revolver, shouting orders.

Mulligan hands me up into the truck. Tilly's body, covered with a blanket, jerks and rolls as the truck clatters over the stony roads.

Slinger's there, eyeing me. 'Good shooting, mate.'

No, it was anger, uncontrolled and burning, forced out of my Bren. A deadly anger, making me into a killing machine. What was it old Rowlands said? 'Blazed away like he was bullet-proof.' Well, that was my dad. Me too? Hell no, I'm not like him.

I'm not like him!

That last bomb caught our ambulance. It's shattered and burning blackly, the greedy, licking flame-noise lost in the clank-clatter of our trucks. We are on the downward road to the coast.

Tilly's arm rolls out. A nice wristwatch and Slinger is eyeing it. He gets my look and eyes it no longer. The others are talking, but not me.

So we are rolling on the coast road now and Lieutenant Creel is wrong. The sea is not wine-dark, it's just grey, and a sharp wind's scudding the wave-tips to white.

Sod all classics.

Webley service revolver

WE ARE ON the quayside of a small Greek town and for once the sky is clear of German birds. Heinkel-birds, Dornier-birds, Junker-birds. There's a big grey destroyer alongside a small jetty. That makes us stop and look, because the Brits don't let their ships out in daylight any more than they have to.

A pile of stuff on the wharf is covered by canvas. Where the covering's pulled off sunlight blinds and flashes. Slinger gives a little moan of wonder, and I swear he smacks his lips.

The Greek government is moving all its gold, keeping it from the Germans. And it is piled up on this jetty, about to be loaded into the destroyer. The destroyer's battered, dented and bullet-marked all over, but the long guns point up into the blue sky.

Gold. In stacks of ingots, canvas bags of coins, gold in long bars and flat sheets, even a dinner-set, complete with knives, all piled there, and it dazzles like the blinding yellow sun. Like sunlight has melted on the quayside.

A naval officer comes running over, shouts to Creel. A brief conference and Creel turns. 'Volunteers to help load the gold — not you, Slinger. Moran, Ernshaw, Bates, catch up with us later.'

We help load the gold. It shimmers and dazzles, and even the little bits are bloody heavy. A bag splits, rolling coins everywhere. The navy troops sweep them up with a broom, whistling. A dozen black-clad Greek officials in bowler hats, gimlet-eyed, glance nervously at the empty blue sky. The head boy has gold fillings in his teeth. He grimaces with anxiety: those gold fillings flash as he glances up at the sky.

The last little canvas bags are carried on board. A navy officer waves us away with shouted thanks. Mooring lines are thrown off and the destroyer heads off, churning to full speed.

We're behind our column now and the Navy types have kindly left some tea and biscuits — and a half-bottle of rum — on the quayside. So we brew up, add the rum, sit and wonder. Even Scoutmaster Bates is open-mouthed.

'What would you do with all that gold?' he mutters.

'Ask Slinger,' I reply, and Ernshaw titters.

One coin is overlooked, a British guinea. I pick it up, flip it into the water. When you might be dead tomorrow, it has no value. Tilly is dead and what price that?

Time to go, and we catch a lift from a late truck. As we do, four Stukas rocket overhead, heading out to sea. After them, lumbering Heinkel torpedo-bombers, following the long-faded wake of the destroyer.

I did read about that destroyer long after. It fought off the Stukas, shooting down two. Then the Heinkels, one of those, too. The destroyer reached Alexandria, listing from near-misses, a few more bomb-splinter marks.

The gold? Enough for a few more shiploads of Yank aeroplanes and tanks — most of which was probably sunk by the U-boats.

And Slinger is strangely matey that night. We get to camp late but he's saved some rations — bully beef and boiled potatoes — and with the artful grin of a conjuror pulling rabbits from a hat — a half-bottle of ouzo. He pours it into our mugs and we look at each other — Slinger being generous? Sudden illness or a near-miss from a bomb?

Concussion can make you do strange things. His grin shows every tobacco-stained fang.

'So what'd you score, boys?'

'Score?' asks Bates, who's already composing a letter to the troop about this.

'You know.' Slinger's evil grin stretches over his yellow teeth. 'All that gold. I hope you scored more than the navy types did.'

'Not me,' I said. 'Those Greek blokes were watching us like hawks.'

'Slinger, that would be dishonest,' says Bates.

Ernshaw, the ex-bank clerk, just chokes on his ouzo, eyes streaming. Slinger doesn't believe it at first, but then just looks at us.

'Well, you blokes are the living end,' he says.

He implies it was practically our duty to get some. That we've blackened the name of the New Zealand Army. That we took his grub under false pretences. He said Aussies would have copped the lot and probably the gold-fillings out of that Greek bloke's teeth. He stalks off into the night, muttering about dozy buggers who don't know their backside from a banjo.

'Even if we had got some,' says Bates, 'there's nothing here to spend it on.'

Forty million, I heard later. A fair bit to get away with, but Slinger would have done his best.

WE'RE NEAR our embarkation port now, caked with dust and bone-tired. Half the boys are down with dysentery, my own guts aching like hell. I keep going because I've got something to prove. Moran, who blazed away at that Stuka. I don't think about that — I think about Tilly's grave with his helmet on top.

Creel, the sly bugger, has got me doing corporal duties, not even mentioning stripes. But we have to keep the blokes together, the Germans are just hours behind.

On the hills, old temples and forts show like big white bones. I move out for a piss, look up to a scuffle of movement. Ernshaw is there, panting and puffing under his pack. He flings it off, clattering rocks away.

'Get back in column,' I growl. A man's entitled to some privacy.

'You know that gold?' he puffs a bit more. 'I did grab a bit.'

'Then get rid of it. They shoot looters.'

Ernshaw pulls out one of those little canvas sacks and two of the little bars. Hell, he was working beside me, I saw nothing! He pitches them among the rocks.

'Slinger would be proud of you,' I say.

Ernshaw, nineteen years old, ledger cadet. These are his true words. 'Slinger? Mum said never go near specimens like him.'

The sun is just too hot for this. 'Ernshaw, you pinched that gold. How does it make you any different?'

'I was taking it in case we needed it, corp.'

'I'm not a corporal. Get moving.'

I boot him back into the column. Late afternoon, I notice he is still staggering a bit. I take him aside, remove another little sack of coins from his pack and chuck them into a ravine.

Ernshaw swore that was the last of it. But a long time later in Cairo, I noticed some nice gold fillings.

It does make you think.

'Hey, Robbie, you awake?'

'Since you shouted in my ear, yes, Mulligan.'

'So we're off tomorrow, then?'

'Today at dawn, two hours, go to bloody sleep.'

'Phyllis, having that kid. She was keen on Neil Carey and he was never slow to hop over fences.'

'Go to sleep, Mulligan.'

'Am I stupid? Do the blokes think I'm stupid, corp?'

'No, they don't. I'm not a corporal. Go to sleep.'

'Then why do they call me "Brick", eh? Brick, thick-as-a-brick, since that letter from Phyllis —'

'Mulligan, it's "brick" because you're a bloody good soldier, as in solid, dependable. And I don't believe your wife jumped into bed with this Carey bloke, the minute your back was turned. Okay?'

'Okay. Thanks, corp.'

'And don't call me corp. Okay — Brick?'

We're all dossing down in a bombed-out warehouse. From the smell, it must've been stacked with sardines when the bombs hit. Not dawn yet but aircraft drone over-head. The German airforce starts early. Mortars are crumping somewhere in the distance; sometimes there's the faraway rattle of a machine-gun.

Embarkation tomorrow and hope like hell the Germans let us go without too much fuss. We've had our bums kicked hard here, but learned how to be soldiers. And I'm not wearing any damned stripes.

I can't get back to sleep. Mulligan, of course, is snoring like a pig.

I FORGET THE name of that port. I remember the gunfire and the dark clouds; buildings shattered like someone punched a fist through them. Gunfire as our rearguard fights the Jerries; fights, knowing they won't get away with us.

Our ship was due at dawn. It comes very late afternoon and we march through the town, past a shattered bank, Greek banknotes fluttering everywhere. Slinger practically drools, but Creel urges us on, gun in hand.

We board the destroyer at dusk. Somewhere white tracer-lines of anti-aircraft fire are climbing slowly into the dark, smoky sky. We are bone-tired, sweating and caked with a week's grime. No food the last two days; that sweetish awful stink of dead bodies in our noses; the flies buzzing everywhere.

We shamble up the jetty, stumble up the swaying gangplank. Ahead of me, Slinger has stuffed all his loot into his kitbag. If he falls in he'll go to the bottom like a stone. A big sailor relieves him of it, with a grin. Mine too, and we go below, packing below-decks. A mug of hot soup and hard navy biscuits. The destroyer shudders and moves; we're jammed in a close mass. The gunfire fades behind us — our rearguard, buying us time with their lives. Mates of mine are in that fading noise.

We get clear. Dusk turns to night and the German

aircraft don't appear — no screaming Stukas or droning Dorniers. They've got plenty of other targets.

Sometime later, I fight my way back onto deck. It's crowded with men, many with no rifles or helmets. The night air is cool on my face and the destroyer shudders under full power, leaving a scrawling phosphorescent wake.

A lot of things are behind me, in the dark. Seaton, who made me a soldier. Tilly, my first real mate. And me, because I'm a changed man. I sense this like I have on a different uniform. I've become a soldier, a good soldier.

So, I should be closer to Old Jacko. I should be understanding him more. No, I still feel a distance. I feel a disturbing anger at what I've seen. A building bewildering fury. Tilly ! Nobody to write to, what the hell would Mum think?

'Jerry won't find us now.' Creel has come up. He offers me a nip from his hipflask and I headshake. 'Moran, you have few vices. Any reason?'

My old man is the reason. Cigarettes, and I think of that coughing yellow phlegm on his stubbled lips. Booze, and I think of his foul beer-stinking breath — *and that time he trampled my chargers! Smashed all my lead soldiers ...*

'What's that?'

I've brought out that Jacko-bullet again. I pass it to Creel and tell him what the scrawled scratches are. He fingers it, passes it back. A total sweat-smelling blackness around us.

'Faith?' he smiles, at least I think he does, in the darkness. 'Faith, as in himself? Or faith in his cause? Or maybe it was ironical.' And in the dark, his eyes narrow, his voice sharpens oddly. 'Moran, what the hell is faith?'

I have no idea. I have never thought that through. So I stick the bullet back in my pocket.

Creel is still talking, looking into the black. 'You know I've got a wife, Moran? Married in Britain, kid on the way. God knows why, maybe trying to prove something —'

Something is happening at the stern. Sailors are forming a line and throwing things overboard. A squawk of protest from the army men is ignored.

'Throwing all the packs overboard,' says Creel. 'Need to lighten ship.'

So our stuff is gone. I'm annoyed a moment, then grin. Can't wait to tell Slinger that his precious loot is overside. 'I'd better get below,' I say.

'Don't tell Slinger till they've finished,' says Creel with a grin.

There are times that bloke can read my mind.

Webley service revolver

Crete, 1941

CRETE IS A big island, shaped a bit like a pork chop. The same hot sunlight and blue skies as Greece; the same brown-eyed, black-haired people. The men with big moustaches, big noses too. The women good-looking in a proud, untouchable way.

Yes, and the men have sharp knives — and a sharper sense of honour. A couple of our blokes tried it on with the local women and have the stitches to prove it.

Mulligan went down to the wine-shop for a few drinks, passed a remark about the barmaid and came back with her white-whiskered old grandad on his heels, waving a long pig sticker.

For a couple of days after that, the trick was to sneak up behind Mulligan and yell in a high voice, 'I keel, I keel!' and watch him jump out of his boots. Slinger tried once too often and got flattened.

We did have time to recover. The Germans needed to, as well. Everyone had gear missing, just about no artillery and mortars. Some replacements came in by ship, but not much.

Our company dug in near Maleme Airfield, because the Jerries would make a dead set for it when they came.

And they were coming.

CREEL ROUNDS us up for one of his talks. The Germans have put an army into North Africa. Take Egypt, cut the Suez Canel and head for the oil states. Best way to take Egypt is to cut supply lines. There's this little island at the bottom of Italy — Malta — supplied from Gibraltar in the west, the Egyptian port of Alexandria at the other end.

The convoys are running now, okay. But if Jerry turns Crete into an airfield — result, no eastbound convoys — Malta will fall, then Egypt. It all sounds so bloody simple — and it means, Creel jokes, we have to hold, even though half of us haven't got a belt to keep our trousers up.

You always laugh when an officer makes a joke.

Then little Ernshaw, always looking for brownie points, pipes up to ask if the *Iliad* is about Crete, too. *Another* twenty minutes about some old king called 'Iddymanus' and his 'black ships' — then a crackpot named Evans, who dug up the ancient palaces a few years ago. Yes, and (Creel rounds off the lecture, beaming) we should go to Knossos and see the ruins. Some bloke called Theseus killed a bull-headed monster there. Slinger mutters something about 'bull'.

We would see this Knossos place but there's too many wine shops on the way. We pass some unkind remarks about Lance-Corporal Ernshaw. He doesn't try giving me orders.

Yes, and I'm up for the Military Medal, getting that Stuka.

Something strange happens.

Near us is a little town, all white-plastered houses and shops huddled together; red-tiled roofs, and doves cooing everywhere. Flocks of the little brown sparrows.

We are dug in our side of the airfield now, slit trenches, some Brens, even a heavy machine-gun. We're ready as we'll ever be. There's a Maori company beside us and a mixed bag of Pom, Aussie and Greek militia on the other side. Most just have their rifles.

The sun shines hot and a calm settles; the rumour now is that Jerry won't come — not after his bloody nose in Greece. We want to believe that, so we do.

Anyway, I'm down there one day in a little wine shop, under a big olive tree, getting outside an omelette, some salt fish, olives and black coffee. Someone plunks themselves down beside me — Creel.

It's a hot day, but his face seems redder than it should be, his voice that bit slurred. Maybe he does take a drink or two, and we don't like officers who do. But Creel was up at the sharp end in Greece and no problems there.

He asks if I want a drink. Yes, I say, coffee. It comes in those little white cups, sloshing into the saucers. Creel pulls a crumpled letter from his pocket, waves it.

'Letter from Dad. Short of everything at home, even wool, and we grow the bloody stuff. Nylon stockings not for love or money, says Mum.' He sips his coffee. 'And we can't get Brens or enough ammo for money — or love.'

'You still think Jerry'll come, sir?'

'No doubt. They've spent time nailing down Greece, but they're ready.'

'The Royal Navy'll stop them.'

Creel has finished his coffee and ordered an ouzo. He rolls an eye at me. 'Maybe.'

It seems the German airforce tangled with a Brit aircraft carrier called *Illustrious* — armoured flight deck, latest design. The Stukas left her a near-sinking scrapyard. And they've been knocking hell out of our convoys since then.

So how will Jerry come, I ask? He closes one eye in a slow wink and orders another ouzo. 'We were briefed on that,' and jabs a finger in the air.

I didn't understand what he meant — then.

He rambles about his old man. His wife in the Wrens, now on pregnancy leave; a rushed marriage. Could have scored a cushy number back in Wellington but wanted to be here — cradle of civilisation, you know?

I'll take your word for it, Mr Creel. I watch as he orders a third ouzo and, not so rambling, asks about my family — my dad.

So I'm talking this time. About hardly ever seeing Jacko — brought up by my mum and relatives. How we scraped through the Depression. Creel looks half-asleep, sipping his drink — but listening. Then he asks a question that he's asked before.

'So, your old man never mentioned my old man?'

I give him the same answer and he nods. But watching me, his lips tighten and he sighs. Then abruptly — almost angrily — asks me about being a corporal.

I tell him to cut my arm off, sleeve and all. That's the only way he'll get the stripes on. Tell him I'm due back, get up to go.

Creel just sits there, watching the doves in the big blue sky.

A week later, things are in the same sleepy hush. I'm at the Maori trenches, training them on the Bren gun. I'm the battalion expert now. They're getting lunch ready and something smells good.

I like them. They're natural fighters, tell me how their grandpas fought the British — roll their eyes and give me a fierce look. I'm glad not to be a German.

One of the sergeants is a big north Auckland guy named Henare Muru. Big — he could break Mulligan across his knee. They've 'liberated' a pig from somewhere and are cooking it in an earth oven.

Jerry aircraft are bombing us now. The rumours of parachutists leave us laughing. Hell, they'd never make it to the ground. Henare and I talk about this as we eat our pork. We reckon all we have to do is present arms and let them land on our bayonets. The pork is good but greasy as hell. My mouth is stuffed — and then suddenly that little tingle comes across me. A prickle like tiny cold pins jabbing all over me.

Henare has already put his plate down, staring upward, nostrils flared. He glances at me, 'You sense it, eh? Fight feeling — enemy?'

A very distant droning and now, in the far distance, tiny rows of bird-specks. In straight lines, getting bigger. Henare has binoculars, hands them to me.

'Lot of the buggers, eh?'

I look through the binoculars. Lines of aircraft in the clear blue sky, fighters wheeling overhead. Those lines of aircraft keep a straight course.

High-level bombing? I line up the nearest slit trench.

Henare grunts, his sweating brown face upturned. He pulls off his wool cap and jams on his helmet. He sniffs, like he can smell something coming.

Now the raid sirens clang, metal on metal, and soldiers run for their slit trenches. The aircraft are over-head but we wait, because this is not usual. We've had bombing raids but nothing like this.

Specks are falling from the planes now, but these are not bombs and they twist somehow — then balloon into tiny white mushrooms. Parachutists!

Henare yells some Maori words that sound very rude. His men are running for their guns, he gives me a shove. 'Come on, Robbie, what're you waiting for — Christmas?'

The parachute troops are lower, as we speak. Now the tac-tac of our guns; black bullet-lines speed skywards. They are dropping, defenceless, looking at our bullets coming up. Some shells burst now, among the aircraft and parachutists. Shouts and gunshots explode around me and Henare's roaring like a bull as he works the bolt of his rifle. More of the big three-engine planes coming over, endless more of those swinging white flowers blossom out.

One or two just keep dropping, the chutes don't open, some swinging limply, others entangled. But more planes come; more and more of those endless tiny white blossoms are drifting down — into the blizzard of tracers streaking up. Lower and lower they come.

'Geeze, they're making it,' yells Henare, and I get a blast of pork and onions on his breath. 'Bayonets, you no-hopers, and try to remember there's a war on!'

We're near an olive grove; the big parachutes are drifting down upon it. Henare runs into it, yelling, a lattice of sunlight and shadows on his face. I follow with the Bren, a dozen guys yelling behind us.

Branches break — the first soldier near ground. Helmeted, camouflage uniform, machine-pistol. The silk cords jerk at him one moment, Henare roars and jabs up with his bayonet. A spurt of blood hits his upturned face, the swinging man kicks, goes limp.

'First fish, first fish!' yells Henare.

Now with a crackle and snapping of branches, the others are down. All around, those drifting white blossoms are suddenly huge parachutes, men coming to earth every-where. The Bren jars as I fire, men collapse and the white silk billows over them. A crashing and ripping sound over-head, ripe olives splotch around me. Boots kicking before me, I angle up the Bren, it stutters, the sound lost in the sudden roar of battle. A machine-pistol falls to the ground.

More are landing, more and more. Now the stutter of their own guns adds to the deadly din. Henare bashes a helmeted head, sticks a second paratrooper. He glares around, screams something, points.

In the field, among scattering sheep, two para-troopers are setting up a machine-gun from the big fallen canisters littered everywhere. I raise the Bren and see my bullets ping off the canisters and hit the troopers. Now firefights, scrambling little battles, are happening all over.

And overhead come more aircraft and they are towing — *towing* — other fat-bellied planes behind them. Planes that have no propellers — gliders! They break loose and begin descending like swollen, stiff-winged birds.

'Geeze, Robbie, these buggers mean business,' grunts Henare as he slams another clip into his Enfield.

One glider lands ahead, lurching clumsily over the field, one wing breaking. I drop to my knee. You can handle the Bren like a sub-machine gun if you are big and strong — I am. It jerks, tac-tac tac-tac, my eyes sting, sweat sticking to my face and my shoulder aching. Louder and louder comes the defending crash of battle, because war has come, battle is joined.

'Robbie!' Henare has found a Thompson sub-machine gun and is blazing away. 'Lotta crap, eh? Lotta crap ahead.'

He's right.

THAT WAS THE first day, and the Germans took Maleme Airport. We took a hell of a toll on their paratroopers but they hung on somehow. And onto the airfield came big lumbering transports, one after the other, unloading more troops.

Yes, and the Stukas — black-outlined, gull-winged memories from Greece. And all their mates — Messerschmitts, Dorniers, Heinkels — getting control of the skies, machine-gunning and bombing us to hell.

We had hit them hard, but we delayed our counter-attack too long and Maleme stayed in their hands. We pushed to the outskirts before being shoved back, finding the bodies of two men whose fighting courage pushed them further than us. Henare was one.

Attack and counter-attack, the green fields littered and burning, the sheep dead, black smoke among the green olive trees. And the stuttering gunfire, startled birds fluttering up. Always more Jerry troops coming and pushing us back. We counter-attacked again, gave them a bloody nose at Galatas. But they were reinforced and kept coming like the tough troops they were.

And they controlled the air. When we weren't fighting, we were dodging bombs. Suda Bay was our main port, and it became a graveyard of burning and sunken ships. With the port itself in ruins, we are pushed further back. And those big transports land like they're on some endless conveyor belt.

And somewhere, a day or so after Galatas, we become the rearguard. Creel's dysentery has returned. He's white and thin, but keeps us moving, shouting encouragement and insults and getting no damned sleep.

Sticking me with corporal duties, even sergeant duties.

And somewhere along the line, still fighting rearguard, our section is cut off.

It's dark. Creel's torch plays a dim yellow on the map, the batteries nearly drained. Lucky, anyway, because even at night the prowling German aircraft will swoop upon every light-point they see.

We are dog-tired, dirty, our uniforms in rags after

the days of fighting, our faces covered with stubble, most of us wounded.

I have a painful cracked rib from diving against a rock when bombed. Slinger has a black-blood bandage around his head, the bottom half of one ear gone. Bates's arm is broken. Mulligan's limping from shell fragments. Harris claims his arm is badly wrenched, can't use his rifle.

I keep an eye on Harris. He's still chocka with this 'Uncle Joe' crap —that because Germany and Russia are allies, he shouldn't really be fighting. And if taken prisoner, Jerry'll send him straight to Russia, the workers' paradise. One foot wrong and I'll send him to another paradise.

Creel still insists on giving me corp duties but we've got Sergeant Dalton from another company and we've picked up some stragglers. Now he switches off the torch and takes a swig of water. 'Cut off,' he murmurs, 'have to detour, to a place on the coast called Sfakis. The Navy's taking off troops there.'

'They won't show their faces,' mutters Harris. I notice a small agreement from the others. 'Jerry'll bomb them to hell and back.'

'The Navy will be there,' says Creel sharply. He knows about Harris. 'And our job is to get there, too.'

Harris is about to reply but I heft the Bren slightly. My shoulder's raw from toting it but I've got three full clips left. He's welcome to them all if he doesn't shut up. He gets the message.

So we go on. And because Bates is wounded, I still have to behave like a corporal. But no way will Creel get those stripes on me. I'm a private and I intend staying as private as hell. Realising I'm Jacko's age, I wonder how quickly he grew up under these same Mediterranean skies.

So we hike towards the coast, keeping under cover because Jerry owns the skies. The big two-engine bombers pass overhead, ignoring us. Not so the Messerschmitts and Stukas, who swoop like hawks.

Once, they see us and we take cover in a vineyard. The Stukas blast it to shredded wood and leaves — but the farmer saves his scowl and shaken fist for the Germans. They'll take Crete but have no fun holding it against people like this.

For two days we hike and there are more bombers overhead. I'm in the rear, just behind Harris and a couple of his mates. Creel drops back for a moment. 'Where're those planes headed, sir?'

'Sfakis,' he says.

Where the navy is taking our boys off. Where Jerry won't make the same mistake as Dunkirk and let an army escape. We don't see that fight and don't hear about it for some time. But the Navy do keep their word — and pay a bloody price in battered and sunk ships all the way from Crete to Egypt.

We don't see it — don't get as far as Sfakis.

On the third day, we hit the coast. There's no food left and Harris is griping worse than ever. We can't see Jerry but know he's close behind. Had to leave two badly wounded men in a village — like signposts, pointing the way.

Bates should have stayed, too. But, ever the scoutmaster, he makes light of his wound, writes another gallant letter to the lads at home. His sandy hair is wet with sweat but his rifle's clean. I don't like the bugger but I have to admire him.

Harris spits. 'We'll never get down that cliff. Jerry's got us pinned now.'

I offer to throw him down. My cracked rib is hurting like hell. Creel peers over, nods. 'We'll work along, find some way to the beach. There's more than one fishing village along here.'

'And what then, sir?' Ernshaw's toting my Bren clips and he's a goner if he loses them. 'We'll still have nowhere to go.'

Harris mutters again but Creel grins, speaking loudly over them. He points. 'We might get a lift on *that*.'

'That' being a long destroyer, black against the blue-grey sea, with a cutting white wake. It's down coast and moving quickly, close to the shore. It'll be up with us in half an hour, Creel estimates.

He's already seen a break in the cliff, a path down to the beach. He raps out orders: Dalton stays with a section. They're to give warning if Jerry comes, and get down quick when the destroyer comes inshore.

If it comes inshore.

Now they're scrambling down and I resist the impulse to boot Harris along faster. Dalton's positioning his men as I look over and see something in the distance — a flash. Someone using binoculars? I borrow Creel's pair and look again, but see nothing. Creel tells Dalton to keep his eyes skinned and we follow.

It's a wide path, with rough steps backed with timber slabs. Leading to a fishing village for sure, shouts Creel as we scramble down. It slopes to more stunted olive trees, and a glimpse of red-tiled roofs through them. And that destroyer is closer, tearing along at full speed.

Even going fast, we're only halfway down when that familiar howl comes out of the blue. Stukas, eight of them, in perfect formation. And behind, a flight of two-engine bombers, long-bodied, perspex heads like blue-bottles.

'Junker 88s,' mutters Creel, white-faced. It's the first time I've heard such sharp despair from him.

Now the destroyer cuts a wide white 'U' in the water as it turns out to sea, the white wake bubbling as it gathers speed. But out of the blue sky come the gull-winged shapes, followed by the long-bodied blue-bottles.

We stand and wait, because that destroyer won't be coming back inshore. Now comes a very distant stutter of gunfire and red streaks of tracer climb lazily towards the attacking aircraft.

The Luftwaffe have lots of practice at this. Both flights split up to attack from different directions. The destroyer twists like a wolf between hawks. Ta-tac-tac, as her guns spit back, mixed with shrill screaming engine-noises.

Creel hands me his binoculars. On the destroyer's crowded decks are men, soldiers, slipping and sliding as the ship wheels. Men like us, scrambling for balance as the long guns arch up and shoot their black bullet-lines. The first bombs fall, black specks we can see easily, tumbling a little, then gathering speed. They miss, sprouting big white wings of water on either side of the black bow. The men cheer but Creel doesn't — mutters that a near-miss can shatter the hull underwater.

Those long-bodied Junkers are swooping now. Guns twinkle in the blue-bottle heads, their engines snarl as more bombs fall. One swerves away, smoke pouring from an engine. Another flips over and into the water, the blue-bottle head shattered by gunfire.

But the destroyer is hit. Still twisting like a long lean black shark, it shudders, smoke pouring from the side. Another near-miss and it heels again, gun still firing. Then a stick of bombs hit it from bow to stern.

Explosions shudder and shake the ship, black smoke and red-orange flame billow up in thick chunky masses. The destroyer's listing over, the black smoke bulking upward. There's a final explosion and the stern rises, the propellers still turning as it slides below and is gone.

A Stuka has smoke pouring from its engine, two black shapes drop away, blooming white parachutes. A yellow life-raft on the water. The other aircraft circle a little then head back to Maleme.

Creel takes a swig from his water-bottle, spits, and rubs a hand over his dirt-grimed face. Then he's recovering, rapping out instructions. We'd better check out this fishing village ahead — no sense heading for the main bay now.

Out to sea, there's only a spreading patch of oil, some debris and maybe bodies. No sign of life. The smoke is drifting away and thinning already.

Bates tears his gaze away from it. Three or four

hundred men dead in as many minutes. 'Sir, maybe we should head for the bay. Our destroyer may come at night.'

Creel shakes his head, his voice quiet. 'I think that *was* our destroyer, old chap.'

THE PATH WINDS through those stunned olive trees. At the end of it, a scatter of little white houses. Villagers, mainly black-clad women and children watch silently as we scramble down towards them. A rickety little jetty juts out to sea and, moored to it, there's a long wooden boat — 'caïques' they are called — with some faded decoration peeling off the sides, a mast laid along the middle and a tattered old sail. It's listing and full of water.

'Our galley!' yells Creel happily. 'Odysseus himself could not wish for more.'

We look at each other. 'Sir,' says Mulligan. 'Nobody likes to give up, but — will that thing get us to Egypt?'

'It's just about sinking and the Germans must be close behind,' says Ernshaw.

'We're entitled to discuss this,' says Harris.

'Of course,' says Creel briskly. 'And I'll shoot the first man who gives me an argument. Harris?'

Harris says nothing. Maybe it's the tone in Creel's voice or my finger sliding around the Bren trigger. Jacko's boy getting caught this early in the war — sod that! Anyway, discussion over.

'Now, let's get our galley launched,' says Creel. 'Black-hulled warships, eh, risking Poseidon's wrath like the stout Ithacan, eh?'

I have no idea what he's talking about. I have no intention of asking him.

Creel gets out the villagers and tries his classical Greek on them. They're mostly women and old men, and he's getting puzzled looks. Then an old man comes strutting out, in a threadbare pinstripe suit that flaps on his skinny body, a grey derby hat jammed firmly on his head. He's holding a battered violin case.

'My name is Andros, captain,' he shouts in American-accented English. 'I'm with you. When those Kraut suckers come, I'll play 'em a tune on my Chicago fiddle.'

Andros was once an American citizen, deported for running boot-leg gin ('I didn't cough enough to the cops'), and now in retirement. He opens the violin case to show his Chicago fiddle. An old Thompson sub-machine gun. Slinger loves him.

The whole village is running around now. The *caïque* mast is raised, a chain of women scoop out the water. The bullet-holes are plugged up. It turns out the men are away, looking for guns to fight the Germans. The problem is, the *caïque* crew is with them. But of course that is no problem for Creel.

He would have won the Junior Wellington Open Yachting, he says, but Vern Leydon cut his wind with an illegal tack that the race umpires must've been blind not to notice.

He's everywhere — so I have to be, thinking that if his dad made Jacko skip like this, no wonder my dad became a good soldier — getting bread and water, even stopping Slinger thieving hens; doing a count, six rifles between the twelve of us, and the Bren. Not much if a Jerry patrol hits us. Or the Stukas find us.

Twice, bombers go overhead and we have to duck for cover. Once, a spindly little aircraft with fixed wheels circles over us as it flies past. Looking for bigger fish — we hope.

'Fieseler Storch spotter,' mutters Creel, who seems to have the name of everything the Germans ever built. 'Don't think he saw anything.'

We hope. The mast is raised, the sail rigged, Creel himself ties the knots. Andros has appointed himself village warden, yelling instructions in a mixture of Greek and American slang. The women ignore him.

'Odysseus made Egypt in about a week,' says Creel to me. 'I'm more or less using the same star-pattern he did.'

Sure, I point out, just don't tell the chaps we're steering to a four-thousand-year-old poem. And does the — ah, *Odyssey* — mention anything about Stukas, Heinkels or Dorniers?

Creel grins, a very tired grin, and his eyes are rimmed red. But the work's done, we're just about ready. Creel sends a runner up to Dalton and our men on the cliff-top, telling him to fall back.

Half an hour, tops, and we'll be on our way.

ANOTHER FLIGHT of German aircraft drones high overhead. Then silence, and in the afternoon heat from somewhere comes every damned fly in Crete. Or maybe we just didn't notice them earlier.

Andros has dismissed the women and old men back to their cottages. He marches up and down the jetty, shouldering his Thompson gun. 'We'll riddle those saps like Swiss cheese,' he says.

Creel tells him several times to remember our patrol will be down first and please not to riddle them. Our patrol. The half hour is up and there's no sign of them.

We sit in the boat, ready to duck under a spare sail if the planes go overhead. The heat comes in thick waves, solid as syrup. The black flies buzz in their clouds; little songbirds call from the olive trees. Clop-clop-clop, Andros marches up and down the jetty.

'Send another man after them?' I ask.

Creel shakes his head. 'Dalton may have them widely spaced. They'll be on their way now.'

But the olive-green slopes are quiet — just those waves of syrupy heat, the buzzing flies and songbirds. Once I hear a faint popping noise and mention it to Creel. We shush everyone and listen. Nothing.

They must be on their way by now.

I'm squatting beside Creel. His head nods, he's near dead with exhaustion. 'Think we've got a chance, sir?'

I get a cheeky grin. 'Of course, Moran. If we don't get bombed, machine-gunned, torpedoed or hit a mine.'

Yeah. I'm getting it now. My Jacko (sometimes I just can't call him 'Dad') just coasted off his officers. Creel's old man must have been bloody good. He blinks again, makes a conscious effort to stay awake.

Moran, I'm recommending you for a medal and sergeant stripes.'

Thanks for nothing — *hell, it did old Jacko no good!*

The afternoon sleeps on — long, leaden, hot moments. Hell, that patrol must be coming. We would have heard something otherwise. Dalton is pulling them back with care, ready for a final scramble.

It's been a lot longer than half an hour now, but we're tired, caught in the sleeping heat of the afternoon. Creel tilts his helmet over his eyes, a black bar of helmet-shadow over his face.

'Moran, my dad used to mention your dad some-times. In his sleep.'

'Sir?'

'He'd shout out, "Moran", then wake up. And his thigh was hurting so much, he'd get up and hobble around. Bad dreams, I don't know. But I'd lie in bed and listen to the endless tap of his cane. I was proud of his MC; you must've been proud of Jacko's VC.'

Jacko hocked the VC for booze. Screw my dad. I'm sweating in the thick syrupy sunshine, the green trees silent. Clop-clop, goes Andros and the flies buzz. Among the olives, the songbirds are silent.

Silence.

There is just a tingle on my sweat-caked skin, just a prickle inside me. So I cock the Bren, Creel is looking up to movement in the tree-line. Andros stops his clop-clopping at the same time, points.

'Ah, your boys come.'

'Andros, get under cover, there's a good fellow,' says Creel quietly. Then to Ernshaw on the docks, 'Cast off the mooring lines.'

Ernshaw does so and jumps aboard. Now there are figures slipping from tree to tree. Dalton, good soldier, won't just walk in. The afternoon shadows are dark and the figures come closer, out into red sunlight flashing on the flat-brimmed helmets. One of them waves.

Our boys. All eight of them.

'Come on, you lazy bludgers,' shouts Creel, with a grin of sheer relief.

They come running out, tunics flapping, heads down against the sunlight. Rifles at the high port — *at the high port!* Tall skinny Dalton, where is he — and Tubby?

'Jerries!' I yell.

Clever bastards — already too close, pulling out machine-pistols, their officer shouting —

Taka-taka-taka-taka, and their officer's spinning around, the men beside him. Old Andros, not so easily fooled, maybe saw the German breeches and boots. Moustache bristling, he blazes away with his Chicago fiddle.

We are firing now and two more Germans go down. The others go to ground. The *caïque* is beginning to swing away, the ancient engine chugging to life.

Andros is running up the jetty, the pinstripe jacket flapping, a hand over his derby hat, his white beard flying. 'Hey, boys, I'm hitching a ride!'

He's at the *caïque* when the bullets hit him, stitching bloodily across that old pinstripe suit. He spins around, the pearl derby flies into the air. Then he pitches over into the water.

Hell! Now we are swinging clear, their bullets cannot sink us; that rage like white-water surging hot,

I'm running to the stern. Creel yells but I ignore him. One of the patrol — oh, how carefully they crept up on Dalton — is about to throw his stick-handled grenade. Tac-tac, and he follows Andros into the water. Explosion, then a big bubble tosses their bodies back up. I whip-lash the Bren along, another falls and the others dive for cover.

Then Creel's shoving me flat, his face red, shouting, 'Moran, I'm bloody sick of slamming you down!'

We're away, but only just. Damned smart to ambush our people and come on in their jackets and helmets. They're still firing from the shoreline, but too bloody late. The afternoon shadows are dark, so it's nearly evening; too bloody late for the Stukas.

We wait for a long hour but the Stukas do not come. Why should they, when half the Royal Navy is a target? We learn later that ten navy ships went down, but most of our blokes were pulled off.

Bloody defeat and no Dunkirk.

We're still in trouble. Bullets hit our water jugs, spouting it everywhere, and there are more problems ahead.

Never mind those Junior Wellington whatevers. The wide blue-grey Mediterranean is different. Away from the shoreline, it's bloody big and empty. Creel's putting on a brave face at the steering but I can tell that the *Odyssey* doesn't make a lot of difference.

'Think I've spent too long among the classics,' he whispers.

The day goes into night, a second day into night. Creel dozes off, exhausted from keeping us together so long. Night again. We drift, although Creel is awake and hauls on the rudder, his face upturned to the stars. The men huddle and Harris inches towards me.

I do not like Harris. I know what he is going to say. I bring the Bren around — one clip left — but he doesn't notice.

'You think I'm a bugger, eh, Moran?'

Yes, I do, and say so.

His stubbled face is close to mine, his breath stinks. 'My dad was a ship's steward. They jammed those guys anywhere. He coughed his lungs into red shit.'

'So —?'

'So the blokes at home write to me and — well, how can I fight for a capitalist system? Easy for them, excused. But I'll do my whack —'

'For Uncle Joe?'

Harris does not reply, and huddles back to the others. But he stood up to the fighting in Greece and Crete, and it makes me think about a different courage.

Here, on the rocking waters Creel is blinking awake. 'Don't know where we are —' His cheeks are thick with stubble and his voice croaks from a dry throat. He looks up at the stars and opens his mouth, sure to begin some crap about the ancient Greeks — then another star bursts overhead.

The star is white and dazzling and floats in the black night air — a flare, showing all our upturned faces, every line of rigging and sail. A man-made star, followed by white tracer blazing over our bows.

A voice calls, broken of identity by the loudspeaker. Not English, harsh and angry. And from nowhere, the black sharp lines of a ship come up from the darkness.

Now a searchlight, yellow and dazzling as the flare, cuts onto our boat. More loudspeaker commands, but Harris, resigned, has it sussed. 'Eyeties. Same as Jerry, eh?'

And Creel, jerking awake, suddenly shouts something in Greek.

There's a shout back, and then urgent commands from the ship as the dazzling searchlight holds us. Creel stands and beams.

'Greek!' he shouts, 'Greek destroyer, bound for Alexandria.'

At the side of that black bulk, the searchlight shows a rope ladder rattling down. An urgent shout does not need translating — move! So our blokes, bone-weary, clamber up.

My turn. 'Sir, did you shout something from the Illy — *Iliad*?'

'The *Odyssey* — now stop smirking and get up that damned ladder.'

Bren gun

Korea, 1951

WHEN IT'S NOT too cold in Korea, then it's too hot. At least, it seems that way to me. Even the scummy brown water of the rice-paddy is hot and little black mozzies buzz everywhere. Human excreta is a fertiliser here and my clothes stink from the little garden I just crawled through. Some wretched farmer's had half his crop spoiled. But he's huddled inside his one-room shack because the big-nose foreign soldiers are here and that means trouble.

So I blink, push the green rice-shoots out of my face and crawl forward, on elbows, knees and hips, my breath stirring the water. I'm damn careful not to swallow any. The bugs kill quicker than bullets.

The sun glares like melting brass. I am stinking, filthy and sweating, my rifle ready because the sniper is ahead some-where. Everyone's gone underground since he arrived. Score, two gunners, a truck driver and a war correspondent who made news the hard way. A few were wounded and the cook had his pots punctured.

He's damned good but we have to winkle him out. Just like old Jacko did with Dead Willi. I read about that duel in the regimental history. A funny name for a sniper, but he was dead enough when Jacko finished with him. He used a Lee Enfield for that duel. I'm using one now with an overbore sight. And I'm stalking a sniper too, but we are no closer. He's still 'Jacko', not Dad. Stop thinking about him — concentrate!

I'm at the other end of the rice-paddy now and my mates by the carrier are making a diversion — I hope. I have belly-snaked more than one mucky hot mile to get here; hope that tricky bugger shows himself.

Never did sniping in Africa. I used to think the heat in the desert was bad enough, then. 'Desert' — funny word because it meant so many things. Sharp black stones in grey earth, stony-ridges. Or the sand-oceans of the Qattara Depression. Tunisia and those fantastic-coloured spring flowers that appeared from nowhere in the spring.

Cairo in Egypt. A hot yellow city, even the dust sparked to gold by the sunlight. Elly. Young Creel and old Creel. Me, still gawky and learning, a better soldier. And the hot steel thunderstorm of El Alamein — thoughts wandering, concentrate!

Eleven long sodding years ago. Now I'm up to the gills in a stinking shit-brown paddy, hunting a killer — who might be hunting me. So concentrate, Robbie, because he will be. And I am on his hunting ground.

Ahead of me is a long hillside where the grass is brown and the rocks stick up like dead grey bones. There's bits of busted equipment everywhere, even burned-out trucks from a battle last year. And the single shrunken carcass of a dead cow, brown hide stretched over a rib-cage, and a skull with horns. It's riddled with bullets from our machine-guns like all the other possible 'hides'.

NO. His 'hide' will be so well hidden that even the little brown songbirds will be fooled.

Movement! *A flicker somewhere in the heat-waves.* Where! *Back up the road, the lads are working on a 'defunct' lorry, clattering away and careful not to show themselves. So forget the painful memories of North Africa. You are here in the stinking warmth, with clouds of mozzies and big blue dragon-flies among them.*

Phut — *the distant faraway shot.*

Hearing it, focusing — firing. One shot, two, three — right at that mummified cow carcass — whose skull-head and horns joggle faintly. 'Cover me!' I yell, and rise out of the stinking muddy water.

Someone shouts, 'Keep down!'

I ignore it. Instinct's guiding me now — that skull-head moved! With steam already rising from my stinking clothes, I'm walking up the hill, pointing the Enfield ahead.

Now the burr-burr of the machine-gun is kicking tufts of dry grass and earth up around the skull-head, shattering it. One of the horns rolls loose.

If I am wrong about the hide then I'm a dead man, walking in the neat sight-lines of a telescopic eye. But I am not wrong. Place a hide somewhere so bloody obvious that nobody will think it's there. Our sniper had real nerve and iron guts. I know I'm right, because I am still alive.

Now the machine-gun stops firing. I walk more carefully because some of these hides are booby-trapped. Already my clothes have dried to just damp, and that stinking mud is plastering my face like a war-mask.

I reach the hide, kick that bullet-shattered skull away and look down. And even for the very clever Chinese and North Koreans, this is very clever.

A manhole, just under the cow's skull itself. He probably shot through the mouth. A narrow shaft of earth, the sniper crouching in the bottom, coming up to fire. Excellent camouflage. I kick open the manhole and take one quick glance.

The sniper is there, shot through the head, brains and blood masking the face like mud plasters mine.

Tears! Is the link between Jacko and me complete, now that I have done his job? Because all those times I was fighting his memory, I was becoming like him? North Africa, Italy, what happened after …

Did he feel this sick taste in victory? That futile waste? Knowing the blokes that do the fighting are never the ones who start it. Harry Truman, Joe Stalin, Mao Zedong — catch them in that manhole.

I pull out a long rifle with Russian lettering down the stock. Damn fine telescopic sights, too. Well, they had plenty of practice on the Germans. I kick the camouflaged manhole-cover shut — somebody else can dig up that mess inside. Or leave it there.

I will keep the rifle. I walk down the slope to the line of men coming up, who stop and look at me, thinking I am a bloody hero. Well, that's all they bloody know.

Lieutenant Gibson hands me his canteen and I empty it. He eyes the rifle. 'Regular army? Bloody good, whoever he was.'

'One out of three,' I reply and walk on down to the carrier, to whistles and a 'good on you, Robbie,' but I ignore those. All I want is a long shower, a hot meal and about two weeks' sleep.

'One out of three,' meaning he was right, about one thing. Gibson will know when he checks that manhole cover.

A regular-army bloke? Well, not a bloke, and looks too young for regular army, maybe fifteen. But she was bloody good.

And I am totally sick of this bloody war that is going bloody nowhere. Just like I am going bloody nowhere.

North Africa went somewhere. Yes, to North Italy. Me and Bates and that bloody mountainside. A girl who wanted to fly like a bird.

Before her, all of bloody North Africa.

North Africa

Egypt, 1941

THE GREEK destroyer gets us into Alexandria at night and we're taken to a big warehouse outside town. Hard floors, just blankets and bully beef stew, but it's heaven. And sleep, asleep all that night and the next day, just waking for meals.

We get kitted out again, even get our mail. Letters from another world, it seems.

Mum writes that Uncle Joseph won a production award for butterfat (news clipping attached) and would I like some socks? Am I going to church and is Crete very hot at this time of year?

Bates's letter is addressed 'Dear Akela.' He explains this is a scout term, quite an important one — so we can jolly well stop laughing. We don't.

Harris gives a satisfied hoot. His waterside mates have struck for more money. And rightly so, he says, the capitalists are making enough.

Some groans. We've heard all this. Germany and Russia have their non-aggression pact and since Russia 'champions the common worker', we shouldn't be fighting for the bankers and merchants who make profits out of our bloodshed.

Uncle Joe, he says (Harris always makes it sound like

he and Stalin are related) is too smart to get drawn into this war — and hats off to any worker who strikes.

Creel has come with the mail. Neat new uniform, polished boots and pink-faced, his arm in a neat black sling. He's walking around the boys, chatting, hears Harris and comes over. There's a very smooth look on his face.

'So, Harris, the workers of the world should not be fighting this war?'

'Capitalists' war, lieutenant, and everyone knows it. That's why Uncle Joe is staying out.'

'Of course,' says Creel very smoothly, 'that non-aggression pact did let Hitler overrun Western Europe without looking over his shoulder.'

'Same reason, lieutenant, capitalist war.'

Creel produces a big white linen handkerchief and wipes his face. Keeps it over his mouth a moment (hiding a smile?) before he speaks again. 'Harris, no man should fight against his principles. You write to Uncle Joe like those Birmingham workers did. And if you get an answer about following your socialist conscience, I'll personally endorse your discharge from the army.'

Every bloke in the warehouse is listening to this now. Creel mops his face again.

Harris looks as suspicious as hell. 'Straight up, sir?'

'My word as an officer and a gentleman.' Creel turns, using his handkerchief to flap at the flies. There's absolute silence as he walks to the warehouse door — then stops and turns.

'Oh, ah … don't expect a quick answer. Uncle Joe's got a slight problem right now. Called Operation Barbarossa.'

'Operation —?'

'Barbarossa.' There's a little smile on Creel's lips. 'Did I neglect to mention that? The German code-name for their attack on Russia. They invaded through Poland a few hours ago. Looks like poor Uncle Joe put his trust in the wrong people.'

He can't resist a wicked grin now as he turns and walks off, khaki shorts flapping around his legs.

Harris is not silent very long. 'Huh! Uncle Joe would've known that! He's trapped Germany, mark my words. He's made this a People's War to save the workers in the west. Hitler's played right into his hands — hey, who threw that boot?'

WE ARE FULLY equipped, better guns and new tanks. 'Honeys', they're nicknamed, because they handle so well. Light-armoured, though, and light-gunned. Seems nobody but Jerry has heard of heavy armour and big guns on tanks. We have some, most at the bottom of the Med.

Malta is getting well and truly hammered. The guy in charge is some holy Joe who spends as much time on his knees as he does working. Convoys get sunk and the ships that do arrive get bombed at the dock. The paratroops — our old mates from Crete — are rumoured to invade. When they do, Malta will fall. Our last lifeline will be cut off and Egypt will be another Greece or Crete. Sure, we have good harbours at Alexandria and Tobruk — full of sunken ships, their funnels sticking out of the water.

The Germans have an army here, the Afrika Korps.

And a general, guy called Rommel, who out-thinks us every time; who bloody seems to know what we're doing; who has pushed our army back to Cairo. They call him the 'Desert Fox'. So this makes our generals a bunch of scared upper-class rabbits. We set up 'boxes', defensive positions; the theory is they will stop the Germans. Of course the Germans might go around them, but maybe our generals didn't think of that.

So we dig into the ground and it's hard as rock. After five minutes swinging a pick, thirst cracks your throat and the sun makes you giddy. This is one time I think about becoming a non-com. At least they're not always on the end of a shovel.

We break at midday for the usual meal. Bully beef that's like soup in the can, from the heat. Jaw-breaking army biscuits spread with jam and — before they reach your mouth — a coating of flies. Brit-style tea, black and so thick with sugar that you can stand a spoon in it.

A Signals Unit is here. Two of their blokes come over, trying to eat and wave off flies at the same time. One sandy-haired guy gives up and throws the tin away. At once, it's covered with a horde of black buzzing flies and he pitches his cup after it. 'Maybe they'll pull us out now,' he growls. 'Sod this place, give it back to the camels.'

Slinger and me look at each other. Slinger gets in first. 'Pull us out — why?'

'Haven't you heard?' says Sandy with an innocent grin. 'Pearl Harbor? The Japs?'

He makes to go, and stops because Mulligan has grabbed his arm. You do stop when Mulligan grabs your arm. When he makes a downward movement, you sit. Sandy sits.

Seems he got it on the short-wave radio. Seems the Japanese have bombed the big American naval base at Pearl Harbor in Hawaii. Half the Yank fleet is sunk. And they're attacking Malaysia, the Philippines, Sumatra — just about everywhere. So all of a sudden, we've got a bigger war than old Jacko ever had; a real 'world war', being fought everywhere. And with all the Australian and New Zealand troops here, what'll stop Japan cleaning up the South Pacific and all of South-East Asia?

Lieutenant Challis poo-poos this. He calls the guys together and lays out some elementary facts.

First of all, just some battleships were sunk at Pearl Harbor, not the aircraft-carriers. And the attack pilots were German, because Intelligence says the Japanese do not make good airmen, and have few modern aircraft.

Second, the Brits are sending a battle fleet — an air-craft-carrier, two battleships and support units — a force big enough to clobber any Jap invasion fleet.

Thirdly, the main Jap target of Malaya will stop them dead. The jungles are impassable and Singapore Island is a fortress ringed by the biggest guns in Asia. Impregnable, he says, cannot be taken.

So we're to sit tight and not worry about the folks at home. The Japs have bitten off more than they can chew, he assures us, and the Yanks will make all the difference — like last time.

Creel (promoted to Captain) is not so sure. The Yanks only just made the difference last time — and this time Germany holds Europe. And he went through Malaya on his way to England and saw the 'impregnable' island of Singapore. So he's not quite as sure as Challis.

CREEL IS RIGHT. By early 1942 the Japanese have just about cleaned up South-East Asia, and the Yanks are on the run in the Pacific. The Japs are bombing Australia and it turns out they can fly their own aircraft — modern designs that can fly rings around ours.

And that Brit battle fleet? Well, the aircraft-carrier went aground on the way and the Jap airforce (manned by Jap pilots) sank the battleships. Yes, and the Jap army got through those not-so-impassable Malayan jungles all right, too.

Singapore, the impregnable island? Well, most of those big guns were fixed to fire out to sea — and the Japs came by land. So Singapore fell and rumour is that one Aussie division is being pulled out — nothing about us, of course.

Captain Creel is a cunning bugger. He tells me things, confides in me, makes me act like a non-com. Those corporal stripes appear by magic on my sleeve.

Slinger says I'll end up like Bates. Ernshaw thinks I should be proud. Harris says it'll go to my head and I needn't think I'm any bloody better than them. Everyone's 'comrade' in Uncle Joe's army. Bates says it's high time I became a non-com. If I'd been a scout, I'd be a sergeant by now — even in line for a commission. Thank God I avoided them.

And Creel goes on a little more about the Japs. Yes, they'll get pushed back when the Yanks are in high gear — when. In 1940, their army was thirty-second on the world list. It'll take a year, two years. His old man is Assoc.-Something Defence and writes that people are scared.

So I have to think about a Japanese army in New Zealand. A Japanese soldier pointing a rifle and bayonet at my mum.

Queer feeling. I've never felt a lot for her, don't even write much. I picture her slopping around in oversize slippers, that baggy cardigan around her shoulders. And for some reason, always think of her shelling peas. Tinkle-tinkle of those shelled peas in the enamel pot. So that night I sit down and write her a long letter. Two pages, long for me. Telling her not to worry, any real trouble and they'll send us back, so not to worry.

It took the Japanese and a whole wide world war to make me write that letter. A couple of days later, I ask Creel if we will be sent home.

No. We have to beat Rommel first. The Australians are sending a division back, but they're a bigger country with more clout. We (and he's quoting Creel senior) are sucking the hind tit. An expression that says it all.

After that, I write to Mum more often.

Devil's eggs grenades

I SAW THE desert as a kid. Saturday matinee flicks, endless waves of sand; the French Foreign Legion in long blue coats and white kepi hats. Yes, and Arabs wrapped in white bathrobes, on camels.

You see, the Italian dictator Mussolini didn't just stuff things up in Greece. He wanted a North African empire like the ancient Romans had. Well, the Brits gave him a bloody nose so, like they did in Greece, the Germans came in — the Afrika Korps and Rommel, the 'Desert Fox'.

Take Egypt and the Suez Canal was the plan. And barrel right through to the oil fields of Arabia and Persia. Then nothing could stop the Germans. But first the desert, Alexandria and Cairo, the big cities of Egypt.

It's not just sand-oceans in this desert — there's a firm coastal strip and a limestone plateau behind it. Most of the fighting is in open country, less than forty miles wide and just right for tanks.

But in the south, the terrain is a right sodding cow. You have the Qattara Depression, three hundred miles of salt marsh. Like a mouldy rice-pudding, a thin crust and bottomless goo beneath. Then the great Libyan desert — you could dump the Indian sub-continent into it — where the wind sweeps sand-dunes up to a thousand feet high. More than a thousand miles on all points of the compass. Sand-seas and a boulder-strewn plain. The Senussi Arabs live here — survive rather, also scorpions and sand-vipers — in sweltering, merciless heat.

This was where we stood and fought. Along the coast, a little rail-siding we would come to know — El

Alamein. Before then, other strange-sounding Arabic names that just spelled blood and death to us.

After training in a big desert camp, we were thrown into the fighting. Rommel was punching it hard and our general was not able to punch back. At one of these strange-sounding names, the war became real and very bloody for us.

Mingar Qaim.

Devil's eggs grenades

It's 4.30 A.M. It is bloody dark and bloody freezing.

Mingar Qaim is a patch of desert. We are trapped here because some bloody general forgot to give the right orders and we have the Afrika Korps around us. Dawn is about one hour away.

And when dawn comes, they will cut us to pieces.

So the plan is that we get out — just before dawn.

Problem is, there's a tight steel ring around us. So, think about a fist hitting armour plate. That'll be us, hitting the German 'Panzer' tanks.

There's one chance, a very slim one. The Germans — and the Italians — won't expect this, we hope. They'll think, say our officers, that we'll dig in and wait for rescue. So we will take them by surprise. We hope.

Our officers are going from group to group, explaining this — and hoping they are making it sound convincing. Some of the men may believe them. In my company, a lot of men do not. Some are scribbling a last message home or writing their wills.

I have taken off my greatcoat and chucked away my blankets. I would rather shiver than be burdened. Stripped my pack too. So I'm bloody cold, but that's better than being bloody dead. Even though chances are I'll be very bloody dead soon enough. Strange to think about death — like it's Mum shelling peas. Like it's doing up boot-laces. Like it's close but somehow pushed away.

I have grenades, my Bren and a canvas belt of spare magazines. Harris is beside me, his breath puffing in white clouds. 'Moran, you know we're stuffed, don't you?'

Bates is on my other side. Hisses to Harris, 'Shut up!'

But we are bloody stuffed. Jerry and his Eytie mates not ready? They are ready and waiting. They'll open us, the first move we make. They have us where they want us. All they have to do is press their triggers.

3.45 a.m. Challis is up with us now, bundled in his greatcoat. Well, that'll just slow you down, mate. He mutters, 'Kick-off in fifteen minutes.'

Kick-off? Did someone smack him with a rugby ball? I check my grenades and spare clips, fifteen endless cold minutes to wait.

It wasn't supposed to be like this. We had thrust up the coast to cut the German road. The problem was,

Rommel didn't want it cut, so he outflanked us and we should have been pulled back. We weren't pulled back and are surrounded. East of us, the Aussies have broken through. We have German and Italian battalions around us. We have their Breda and Spandau machine-guns. Their nasty PAK-45mm and their big 88mm. They are waiting, wide-awake, and let nobody tell me they are not. They will start shooting and mow us down.

A fist hitting armour plate.

I have a last tin of bully beef, scrape scrape as I open it, one last biscuit. I drink the last of my canteen and my swallowing sounds too loud.

Jacko, you felt this. Did you feel my cold wretched anger? Because screw our stupid brass who landed us in this — who will tut-tut as the casualty reports come in.

Casualty Bates, who's a damn good non-com. Who's grinning at me because good non-coms do.

Casualty Ernshaw, lying flat, his rifle pushed out in front, his eyes slitted and lips pressed tight.

Casualties Slinger and Harris. Slinger looks asleep, fag in the corner of his mouth. Harris belches and runs a finger down the barrel of his Enfield. Since Barbarossa, he likes killing Germans.

3.50 a.m. Times like these, I don't like being Jacko's boy. I'm expected to be better, be a bloody hero; that is far from my thoughts. A thick stubble on my chin, the stones sharp under my elbows, the Bren strap cutting my shoulder. I'm thinking about that. How it is still black, and freezing men are shifting and muttering. A cold little wind is blowing sand into our faces.

Challis is back, leans over. 'Your section leads, Moran. Whatever you hit, just keep going.' All this in a low voice.

I nod. What are you whispering for, Lieutenant Challis? We could have a brass band playing 'God Save the King' without giving anything away. The Aussies broke out, that'll have tipped them off. They're ready, sipping their revolting 'black-sweat' coffee, puffing their own breath over their machine-gun breeches.

They won't be scared. Nicely dug in behind trenches and rock-pile sangars. All they have to do is wait, press the trigger and start killing.

'Just keep going,' he repeats, and moves on.

I say 'yes', and he waits, so I add a 'sir'. Whatever we hit? Like those well-armoured big-gunned Panzer tanks? Or those new all-alloy machine-guns, the M42, no jamming, firing some fifteen hundred bullets a minute?

Challis goes on. I wish Creel was here, he's got the knack of getting blokes going. But he's off on a training course, the lucky sod. Well, he'd just get himself killed, probably, shouting something from those 'epic poems' he's always rattling on about.

'Minute to four,' mutters Bates.

I think Slinger is actually asleep. I nudge him, he opens his eyes and yawns.

Less than a minute. Everywhere in the desert, in all bloody North Africa, there are tiny sharp stones waiting to jab you. They jab me as I shift the Bren around. In the very far distance, is a faint suggestion of pink. Arabs say that the dawn comes when you can tell a black thread from a white one. We're a long way off that.

4.00 a.m. We're all getting up and I force my frozen body into movement. Swing the Bren to the front and walk forward. Crunch, crunch, crunch, all along the line — we might as well *broadcast* … The shuffling of our footsteps, stones clinked aside, muttered curses, a clash as one man trips. The clank and clatter of weapons, the click-click of bolts pulled back. We walk into the darkness — *hell, are they deaf!*

No, they are not deaf. My eyes water in the blasting cold, the sand is thick on my lips, the Bren like ice. No, they are waiting for us, in their tanks and sangars, behind their brand-new machine-guns. Fifteen hundred rounds a minute? Yes, and those Italian Bredas are bloody fast too.

We are all shuffling faster, mutters and panting around me. Can't stop, boots clumping on those sharp stones, I'm glaring into the darkness ahead — *so open fire, you bastards!*

A rifle shot, one of ours, makes me flinch. Another clash, another man goes over. Ahead, a yell in German. A shot, a flare bursts dazzling white overhead, another shot; then a scatter and run, run because that is not ambush fire. That's not a rapid-fire grid blazing off! Incredibly, that is half-asleep men getting booted awake. More flares burst overhead. I am yelling and it's taken up along our line.

Surprise — we caught them by surprise!

And we're hitting their front sangars, kicking the stones over. A man rises, tat-tat goes my Bren, he's flung back, my boot hits his face. Beside me, Slinger screams, bayonet out and his eyes slitted.

Machine-guns now, and bigger guns, chatter and explode, but we have hit them and are through, like a storming half-caught wave, but still sweeping on. Tents are kicked over, shirt-sleeved figures scramble out — falling. More flares whiten up the shadow-caught darkness. The long vicious chatter of a machine-gun catches eight men in the blast.

Where is it! Fumbling for a grenade — why does old O'Brian spring to mind, cricket-coach, *Put your body into it, Moran* — I throw it at the humped sangars ahead. I'm still running as the explosion hits me — my cheeks sting. A German helmet spins upended. I boot it away. The machine-gun has two men sprawled over it.

Keep going — *keep going!* Into the darkness … there's a deafening rattle of gunfire now, but not the volleys we were dreading. So it comes to us, sweeping like an icy blazing wave from man to man.

Caught them flatfooted — *impossible, but we did!*

A small *kubelwagen* lurches sideways, burning. Another bigger black shape — hell, a tank — no, a lorry. A grenade explodes, it overturns, throwing out a tangle of men, we boot and club them. Orange-dark flames come from the bonnet … hell-fire and hell-smoke around us. Overhead, red, white and green flares light ghastly dawn light. Our charge is a black moving shape, torn from darkness. There's a stench of oil, burning flesh and bitter stinging gunsmoke. Screams … and running into the flare light, I can feel Jacko's old bad fire —

'Come on, you bludgers!'

There are Germans ahead, an officer yelling to his men. Tac-tac-tac, goes my Bren, grenades explode around them. A scream, a man staggers, arm torn off at the shoulder. Bending to pick it up with the other hand, he's kicked, trampled as we go over.

You kicked my little lead soldiers … thinking of something like this, I …

Trucks ahead brake hard, spilling out Panzer grenadiers, tough storm-troops. Grenades. I bash a new clip on the Bren, a man looming ahead. Hell, his bayonet is coming at me — Slinger shoots him, screaming with gut-fired hate. *Thanks, Slinger!* I pull back the cocking lever on the Bren, oddly staggering a moment. Then on, on into the storming, red-fired, half light.

Now an armoured car humps up, a machine-gunner and the driver behind iron slits. It rolls towards us, spitting bullets, blokes go to ground, our rush falters.

NO — that is death!

That new clip's on the Bren. I'm standing up, cold in mind and body, as the black bullet-spitting shape roars up. The Bren stutters and sparks glance red off the armour-plate, around the vision slit. Now the armoured car swerves and blunders, a dead or wounded hand at the wheel.

I shift target to the machine-gunner. He collapses back, the armoured car stops. A strange slow-clicking fire in me, I run forward, up onto a battered mudguard and drop a grenade through the open hatch.

I'm thrown off, winded by the explosion. Ernshaw hauls me up. The armoured car lurches more steeply, one set of wheels spinning, black smoke in the half-light. There's blood on me, sticky and warm.

Jerry is caught but still full of fight. Yelling, I push on, *on* into the weird flare light, the gunsmoke and gun-fire, the creeping pale dawn. I am filthy, coughing gunsmoke, my shoulder aching red-hot. I am staggering on legs like jelly, my face a thick sand mask. My ribs jab a red-hot savage pain when I move. But Jacko's fire makes me charge forward on wobbly legs, shouting loud noise through my thick dry lips, eyes watering in that damned fire and smoke — and suddenly we are through, all down the line.

All down the line, and I'll never know how, but we did crack them. Led by heroes like Captain Charles Upham, a man truly without fear; he bombed and gunned through, taking on a truckload of grenadiers. I bet he didn't feel that hot-cold fire or my doubts and anger. I bet he did not rage at his dad in the heat of combat. I did, and that does not make me a bloody hero.

So I hate these corporal stripes and hate the looks I get when later that morning we stop and brew up. Like I'm a hero, which is crap. If they knew about that ice-hot rage — *hell, he stamped on my chargers* — they'd know my heroics were fraud. Stinking sweat and sand-plastered fraud, a warm caking muck on my face. My hands are trembling as I clip on the last Bren magazine.

Slinger has found a tin of condensed milk somewhere — Slinger would find brandy in a temperance hotel. It muddies the water yellow, and Bates has a bottle of schnapps found in a tent he kicked over. I hope the scouts never find out. Odd-smelling muck and the best thing we ever tasted.

Challis comes up, his wrist wrapped in a field-dressing, his jaw caked with black blood. He has lost his greatcoat somewhere, but is grinning like his team has won a match. 'Moran, you were great.' Like I'd scored a winning kick in the finals. 'First class.'

That warm caked muck on my face is drying blood. I sip the evil-tasting hot liquid. My ribs are bruised — colliding with that armoured car. A bullet has scored past my lower leg, caking my boot with blood. Dried blood cracks on my face as I glower around.

They shouldn't look at me like I'm that comic-guy, Superman. And why does Challis grin and send a medic to me? Jacko's fire — *hell, Challis, you never had a dad like him!*

'I'm all right.'

It's no more than the truth. I can go a good way yet. But the noise of battle is dying away and we are out of Mingar Qaim. Another defeat, though. If the Germans take Cairo, then the war here is over.

The bloody Afrika Korps is closer — and stronger — than ever. But they won't forget Mingar Qaim.

Bren gun

ARMY WORK is routine — even patrols, learning the mine-field layout, keeping well clear of the German positions, checking them for movement. And paperwork, bloody paperwork that makes me wish I was a private again.

There are times that stick in your mind. Little things like dead flies in a cobweb …

We're on this long-range patrol once. Two days out into the Qattara depression, endless square miles of sand-sea that you just cannot make mistakes in. Some do, and stay there forever. On this patrol, we're moving around one of our minefields (millions of them, planted on both sides) to check whether Jerry is moving this way. Aerial recon-naissance spotted their vehicles. So we are moving towards them, two jeeps, into a sand-wind blasting like buck-shot.

On the second day we stop. There's no sign of any-thing German and we curse the stupid bloody pilot who just saw one sand-dune too many. We post sentries and sleep. The wind stops; overhead is the clear, fantastic, night sky. We never saw this many stars at home. Thank God, Captain Creel isn't here to bore the crap out of us about constellations. Just stars, in dazzling patterns and shoals, like black water has swished millions of tiny diamonds into the night. Looking up at the bottomless diamond ocean you could keep tumbling until the black end of time.

I woke early — with an instinct of danger in the freezing dark shadows. Dawn is a faint trace of pink and the stars are gone. Utter stillness. I stand up, grabbing the Bren. Our sentries are out, good lads, on the alert. I look around — *how come they never saw that?*

On a sand dune like a sharp sweeping wave is a

German machine-gunner and loader, about a hundred yards away. A German officer is kneeling with binoculars — waiting for us to wake up! The way that gun's placed, we'll be dead in seconds. But they haven't yelled at us to surrender — or opened up. A sentry has seen them, makes to shout. I stop him. I know why the Jerries haven't moved.

I walk towards the machine-gun with my Bren still ready, but every step telling me I'm right about them; why the gun doesn't seem to be quite pointing at us; why the three men don't move; or the officer, his head cocked.

They're dead. They've been dead a long time, maybe since last summer. Battle swirled this way then. I get to them.

The gunner's flat behind his gun but face-down in the sand, one hand — a wrinkled brown claw — on the gun, a belt of ammunition hooked and ready. The loader is beside him, and a tin ammo case open and dented with the same bullets that killed them both.

And that officer kneels with his head cocked; his sand-goggles pushed back on his cap; his brown skin baked over his skull-face, sand in the sockets of his eyes; lips shrivelled back over grinning teeth. His uniform rags still flap to the same wind that blew away their sand cover.

They were almost certainly killed by an air-strike and sun-baked hard and stiff. Beyond them in a drift of sand are other bodies. Claw hands clutch out of the sand, more skull faces with sand-clogged mouth and eye sockets. Baked each day and frozen each night.

A strong patrol this, and maybe waiting in ambush when our fighters saw them. Bombs first, then a few strafing passes would have finished off the survivors. There's a *kubelwagen*, the paint blistered and blasted by sand and wind, with a headless driver sitting behind a shattered windscreen, sand-goggles around his neck; a truck, the tarpaulin now paper-thin rags. Men — things that were once men — lie in the drifting sand.

All of us are up now, walking among the bodies, all maybe thinking the same thing: these were men like us. Family, wives and sweethearts may know they're dead — but don't know they're dead like this. We will leave them there. There are too many to bury and, anyway, Challis murmurs, the desert will take them to itself. Maybe in a couple of thousand years, it will uncover them again; somebody will find them and wonder.

I gently pull the M-42 free from the gunner. His dry fingers snap like brown sticks, a horrible little sound. I turn the gun over, blow the sand clear. The machine-gun belt tinkles as the others watch. I press the trigger. I'm braced, just five shots, but the gun jumps alive in my hand. Tack-tack-tack-tack-tack, loud and brief in the still air. Challis whistles. All of them get the idea.

After maybe twelve months in the open, my Bren would be a rust-block. That alloy construction does work. I chuck it in the back of our truck.

Nobody has said much and nobody wants to; much less touch them, go through their pockets. Challis gets some tattered maps from the *kubelwagen*. It could have been us out there, all these months.

The wind is up again as our trucks leave. The loud noise of our engines seems indecent. I look back once.

On the ridge, the officer still watches us before a sand-flurry hides him from view.

When we tell him Creel is unsurprised. According to Herodotus (whoever he was) the king of Assyria (wherever that was) sent an army of fifty thousand men into the desert. They're still there — somewhere. Like those Jerries.

And he's already talking about making me sergeant. Creel that is, not Herodotus.

THE BEDFORD bogs again — they are sods in the soft desert sand — and Slinger jumps down, yelling for some of the prisoners to help push. The engine revs, the sand clouds rise, those million black flies swirl. The truck bumps and is pushed onto harder roadside ground. Even that makes the sweat run and Slinger yells for water.

The Italians don't get any; we haven't got enough. There's about two hundred of them, rounded up by our tanks. No water is the reason they surrendered. It'll be a couple of hours trudge before they get any. So they trudge on, sanded to a desert grime, uniforms oil-smudged. Our guards finger their rifles, because none have been properly searched yet. It can wait. Hunger and thirst have knocked the fight out of them — as it would anyone.

'Poor buggers'd give their right arms for a mouthful of water,' mutters Bates, as we get back into the truck.

Slinger has joined us and runs his tongue over his yellow teeth. '*Acqua.* That Eyetie for water, sarge?'

Bates nods. Slinger whistles and disappears.

So we take a swig each from the big canvas sacks; have to ignore the pleading eyes from the line of shambling dust-caked men. Now Dodd appears (Slinger's mate, so he needs watching) and says the engine's knocking a bit. Spark-plugs; he'll need ten minutes, all right? Bates nods.

The prisoners go on and on. They're young, most of them conscripts, but we don't believe our own propaganda about Italian troops. Bersaglieri and Fogliore are good; anyone who's tangled with the Ariete Division has a fight on their hands. Sure, some of their equipment is crap — some of it's bloody good.

Bates is opening a couple of tins with his bayonet. Eyetie rations we picked up. I look at the open tin. 'A.M.?' It's a kind of sausage meat. 'What the hell does that stand for?'

Dodd calls from the engine. 'Some Eyetie told me it stood for *Arabo Morto*, corp.'

'Which means?'

'Dead Arab.'

He disappears behind the bonnet again. I put down the can and curse like hell. An army jeep is coming, full of peaked caps. Probably want to know why we're stopped. It stops and I breathe a sigh of relief.

It's Cotterell, the padre, nice enough guy and (for an officer) harmless. He wanders around and comes up to Bates, smiling. Of course, he was in the damned scouts, too. 'Good result, eh, sergeant? A few more in the bag, what?'

'Sir,' says Bates.

I say nothing. Hope our bloke doesn't turn round

and ask when I last had confession, because I can't remember. Religion is Mum's big thing, not mine. The padre wanders around the truck; even Dodd talks to him for a few minutes until my boot hits his mudguard.

Cotterell's about to get back in the jeep and turns to nod at Bates and me. 'Good men in your section, sergeant. Christ-like — yes, fine Christians all.'

He gets in and the jeep drives on down the shambling, weary line. Bates and I just look at each other. Fine Christians all? Two of our blokes are Slinger and Dodd — Christ-like?

I walk around the open bonnet. Dodd hurriedly begins to tinker but I've seen the fag. I walk down to the back of the truck. Slinger is nowhere to be seen and neither is the second water bag.

Slinger's about ten yards down the line, water bag in one hand, calling, '*Acqua, acqua,*' then a couple of other words. As I come up, an Italian officer drops out, his chin heavy with black stubble. He gets a drink, hands something over.

'Slinger, you utter ratbag.'

He jumps a little but the big innocent look is firmly in place when he turns. 'Oh, hi, sarge, just giving these poor lads a drop of water.'

His big innocent look and big innocent tone of voice may have fooled the padre but 'Christ-like' Slinger doesn't fool me. I jerk my thumb back at the truck.

Slinger empties his loot on the tailboard. Half a dozen expensive-looking watches, a couple of gold cigarette cases, signet-rings, even a silver crucifix. I stare him down and he pulls out another cigarette case, a diamond tie-pin, gold cufflinks and a silver-mounted comb, a couple of silver cigarette-lighters and a dagger, studded with gemstones.

'Is that all?'

'Yes, corp.'

It's not. But Slinger is a mate and I need him. The best stuff is hidden in those damn deep pockets of his. I sweep the pile off the tailboard and kick sand over it. I tell Dodd that engine had better be ready now, and it is. I swear Slinger grabbed some stuff back up when I turned.

Bates takes his turn in the back. Slinger joins me in the cab and takes the wheel. We bump back into the road and the shuffling lines make room for us.

'*Acqua*. Italian for water. I should have bloody known.'

'What tripped me up, Robbie?'

'Cracking on to the padre about being Christ-like.'

Slinger nods, a mistake, won't happen again. He makes to offer me a nip of brandy then remembers he's not supposed to own a silver hip-flask. I pretend not to see it.

'Bet you know the Eyetie for silver and gold, eh?'

'*Argento* and *oro*, corp.'

The truck swerves past another patch of soft sand and the line scatters again. Extra duties will wipe that stupid grin off Slinger's face. I growl, still not looking at him.

'Slinger, you are the worst bloody bludger and biggest bloody thief in the entire Eighth Army.'

Slinger is whistling 'Lili Marlene'. He breaks off, managing to sound very injured and not a little offended. 'You don't know that many Australians, do you Robbie?'

I tell him to shut up and drive. It's that or kick him out of the cab.

THIS TIME we're in a truck, heading back to the depot with wounded men inside, some hurt badly, who need treatment at once. Mulligan's among them — his lower leg shattered, a tourniquet above the knee. Jerry laid down a damned accurate mortar stonk and I'm bashed about, myself, and aching like hell from bruised ribs, so I get the duty with Bates.

Bates is driving and, as usual, chattering about his scouts. They're collecting scrap, running messages; doing every patriotic thing they can think of and still helping old ladies across the road.

I'd rather be home helping old ladies across the road, too. But I'm on a rutted desert road, full of dust and bumping so bad I'm waiting for an axle to break. And I think we are lost.

It's another of those bloody little fights where Jerry pushes in and we have to push him out. Old Jacko's war had frontlines, ours does not, in battle. There are other trucks ahead, so we head for them. Slowly, in case they are Jerry.

'Bedfords,' says Bates, with a sigh. 'Yes, and one of our Valentines.'

The trucks and tank are unmistakable. We pass them

and pull up on the other side. Bates spits. 'Hope they can point us —'

He stops because I've grabbed his arm. I whip off my helmet, tip his over onto his lap and point with my thumb. Because the trucks and tanks may be ours but the guys beside them are not. Tan uniforms, neat little forage caps and *Schmeissers* over the shoulder. And we don't stencil black crosses on our vehicles.

'Jerry?' says Bates.

'You don't miss a thing, do you?' I snap.

Jerry uses our vehicles. We use their stuff too, but they're masters at it — trucks, jeeps, even tanks. And now the soldiers are looking at us. We're just two shirt-sleeved sunburned blokes, so far. 'Wave at them,' I hiss. 'Light up, look natural.'

'I don't smoke.'

I don't either. Nearly every soldier does, so two non-smokers will stick out like we're ten feet tall and painted purple. But I have some cigarettes for the blokes in the back. So with fags wobbling in our mouths, I mutter to Bates to U-turn and head back the way we came. A couple of Hurricanes streak low overhead. Thank God, they don't try to shoot us.

So we're turned, heading back to the Jerry Bedfords and Valentine. One puts up a hand to stop us. He has a machine-pistol in the other hand, so I do. We stop and he strolls up. Blue eyes, brown-tanned face and a bristly fair stubble. Uniform torn and oil-stained, tunic open to the waist.

He looks in the back, sees white-faced men and red

bandages, a huddle of blankets. Saunters up to us, unlit cigarette bobbing in his mouth. He jabbers something at us. Waits for an answer.

This should be the end. But I can be inspired sometimes. That unlit cigarette, the question in his voice. I hand him a box of matches. He takes it, says something and jerks his thumb. We drive off, expecting to be riddled with bullets. Nothing, so we accelerate and, a mile down, hit one of our checkpoints.

'Bloody close,' says Bates.

I'm thinking about that Jerry's last words. One of them sounded like 'Tommi'. Maybe they were awake to us; maybe just wanted to drink their 'black-sweat' coffee in peace — not be lumbered with prisoners.

Bates is still tense. I tell him that the top Jerry, Rommel, once toured a frontline casualty station by accident. Realised it was one of ours and lammed out quick. I get a suspicious look because I'm so straight-faced. But I nod. Bates thinks a moment. 'Nobody noticed he was speaking German?

'They thought he was Polish.'

I get another look from Bates. But it's true. We're always mixing like this. I wonder if those Jerries did let us through.

It's not at all like old Jacko's war.

Webley service revolver

THERE'S A muck-up over stores and Creel uses the excuse to go into Cairo overnight. He takes me and young Harvey, the new company clerk, with him. We can drop in and see Mulligan in hospital.

Harvey stays with the jeep, otherwise it will vanish. It's a big super-clean hospital, starchy white-clad nurses everywhere. Lucky Creel is here, otherwise it would be 'Sod off, sergeant. Not visiting hours.'

Yes, 'sergeant'. Creel finally pressured me into putting them on, the dedicated bugger. The blokes reckon he put a gun to my head.

We find Mulligan in a ward with about sixty others. He's white-faced and still looks knocked to hell. His collarbone's reset so that his arm is plastered up in a crazy salute, his lower body and legs are covered with a neat framework of blankets. He grins, pleased to see us. I give him chocolate; he says he's dying for an En-Zed beer. Wrong choice of words, grins Creel. Should be living for one.

We chat a minute or so but he's in real pain. Will be shipped home, back to the sheep-farm and running after dogs. He stirs a little, can we tuck in his left foot — it's bloody cold.

I lift the blanket, but there is no foot, no leg under the knee. Creel flickers his eyelid in warning. Mulligan's too weak for bad news. There's a catch in Creel's voice as he speaks. 'We'll be back soon, Mulligan. I'll write to your folks.'

We go then. I'm only just holding myself together. Mulligan was fullback for his province rugby team, a cert for the All Blacks tour. But there wasn't one in 1940. And he won't be in the next one, now.

Outside the hospital there's all the stink and crowded bustle of Cairo. Right beside us, a thin gharry horse drops its load and a million black flies home in. Creel sweats, mopping his brow. Says he's got some paperwork to sort out, will need Harvey. I'm free. We'll meet up tomorrow morning.

He and Harvey drive off. I'm not that innocent, I can guess what 'paperwork' means, but it's not my business. A hostel, a decent meal and bed is all I want. So I hop in the gharry and the driver takes me by the shortest route — must be new to the job.

Lots of volunteers run these hostels, mostly middle-aged ladies in grey skirts and white blouses. This one's run by a grey-haired dragon who looks like she's overdosed on Epsom Salts. I bump into one as I go in, nearly knocking her over. But she's young and pretty, with short black hair in that wartime style. I apologise and she smiles.

'Touch me there again and you'll have to marry me.'

We're lectured a lot about wartime morals. Back in New Zealand, if a girl said that, her dad and her brothers would lock her in the bedroom. She laughs, nice blue eyes already noting my medal ribbon, and introduces herself, Eleanor Wyndham-Ffoukes. She gets me signed in, a nice bed near the showers — breakfast at seven — and she even walks up the steps to the first floor with me, still smiling as she shows me the room, big and long with ornate plaster ceilings. Always some little white specks falling.

I dump my kit and she turns and heads off. I've never been one for the ladies — not many chances when you live with Mum and go to an all-boys church school. Sex education — just take cold showers, lads. She's class, double-barrelled surname, I'd be mad to —

'Hey, miss.'

She turns, her face smooth. I walk down to her, aware how my big boots clop. I'm clumsy as hell. There's a little amused smile on her lips now. My face is going red. I take a deep breath.

'Ah, miss, listen … if I'm not cutting some bloke out … maybe have dinner or a drink … just if you're not busy, expect you are … um?'

She gives that little cool smile and I freeze. She'll brush me off, even snub me. But she just smiles and nods, six p.m. in the foyer? She turns to go. I ask if she knows somewhere that serves decent grub.

'Decent grub, sergeant? Oh yes, one or two places.'

She pulls me into the Trocadero — big place with glass chandeliers, a few too many officers for my liking. She just pouts, hates all that stuffy class stuff that Mummy's always lecturing her on.

'*Honi soit qui mal y pense*, poppet. Evil to him who evil thinks.'

She's different. She listens to me talk about the war, notes that I don't talk much about home. She eases that out of me, too, and I find myself talking about old Jacko. She even nods sympathetically. 'My pop survived the trenches. Never talked about it, shot himself cleaning his gun for the Glorious Fourth. Accident — they said.'

I show her the 'Faith' bullet. I hardly ever show that to anyone.

'You are close to him, Robbie. At least you want to be. Otherwise why carry this?'

I stick it back in my pocket. An officer pauses at our table, slim, hand-tailored uniform and long moustaches. His hat's under his arm, so I don't salute. He flicks a cold look at me like I'm a bug squashed on the windscreen.

He addresses Eleanor as 'Elly'. He talked to Lady Bourchier today (Epsom Salts); did Elly know her brother's regiment is back in Cairo? After another cold flick of his eyes at me, he goes.

Eleanor smiles. 'Cherrypicker — they're all frightfully up themselves.'

Her brother's in the same regiment, Eleventh Hussars. 'Cherrypickers' because in some war (about two hundred years ago) they were ambushed in a fruit orchard by French Cavalry and sent packing. Hence the nickname. She says the Brit army is riddled with silly traditions and that's why nobody likes Monty — Bernard Law Montgomery, tipped for command here.

She raises her eyebrows when I ask why. 'Because he damns stupid army convention, Robbie. Also he's bloody good and that's bloody inexcusable.'

She leans her elbows on the table and picks at her peach melba. She actually looks thoughtful. 'He knows this new civilian army won't fight just for King and Country. Their fathers died in the first lot for that little cliché. They want to know why, and all the fox-hunting and jolly hockey-sticks crap impresses them not at all.' She smiles at the look on my face. 'Oh, Robbie, half the bloody upper-class are pro-Hitler. Do you think Churchill's got the entire party behind him? Half of them would stab him in the back, first chance they got.'

Royal family, top politicians, nobody wanted this war. Her uncle in the Foreign Office gives her the goss. They were trying to work a truce with Hitler before France fell; that the Reds will score big-time; that the Empire will go, because the Japanese have destroyed the myth of white supremacy.

Then she laughs, suddenly irreverent and joking. Tells me to call her 'Elly' or she'll slosh me with her dessert. We walk back to the hostel and she warns me not to get serious. She gets regular 'officers-only' lectures from Epsom Salts.

'I'm a flibberty-gibbert, Robbie, not approved of at all. Being seen with a non-com is like being caught laughing in church.'

Plaster is peeling off the columns of that big doorway. She pulls me into an alcove with a pot-plant the size of a palm-tree. Some insect drops on my head but the kiss is worth it. Then we're in the foyer and, for the benefit of Lady Bourchier, who's hovering, she gives me a demure smile and a polite, 'Thank you for a lovely evening, sergeant. All the best.'

Judging from her looks, Epsom Salts is not fooled. Elly whispers, then goes inside. I go outside, that whisper still in my ear. She wants to see me again.

I see my first American non-com in Cairo, too, leaning on the bonnet of a long black Ford, a thick cigar in one corner of his mouth. He's tall, his face blistered red by the sun, good uniform, puttees and boots, his cap pushed sideways. He addresses me as 'Mac'. 'Mac, got an Iron Cross? Promised me kid brother one of them Heimie medals. Worth a fin for the real McCoy.'

We get talking and he gives me a long flat stick of gum. He's driving officers around; they're 'getting the low-down, sort of taking a hinge on this situation'. Yeah, and we Limeys can stop sweating because Uncle Sam'll kick the cactus out of 'dese krauts', see if they don't.

The difference between Limeys and Kiwis is lost on him. (Noo Zeelun — where's that little piece of real estate?) Back home, half the guys are drilling with broomsticks — so it's going to be a little time before they invite Hitler to an ass-kicking party.

Yeah, and that Jap, Tojo, he got an invite too. And the fat guy Mussolini. First they gotta clean up the Nip Navy, gonna need new warships, maybe a million. Airplanes too, maybe a million. On account they sent most of their stuff to Churchill and the Kraut subs deep-sixed it. Tanks too, maybe a million — the tin cans they got now are strictly purple-heart wagons.

So when, I ask, are they coming?

'Search me, Bud.'

He gives me a cigar, 'genuine nickel stogie'. He's William J. Schuyler (Dad immigrated from Kraut-land) and stuck for the duration. Army pay stinks (three times what we're getting) and they done slapped a PFC on him. Private First Class (he grins) but his wiseacre mates say it means 'Praying For Civilian'. Everyone's a wisenheimer.

His officers come out. No salute, just, 'Where now, loot?' and, 'So long, Bud' as he gets back into the car. But he comes across as solid, confident. If they're all like him, they'll be all right.

Slinger's eyes go out on stalks when I tell him what Yanks are paid. It turns out a 'fin' is twenty dollars and he has a bagful of Iron Crosses. He groans, heart-broken, then brightens up. There'll be more Yanks coming over, do I know how many?

'Search me, Bud. Maybe a million.'

British PIAT gun

IN ONE OF those sharp little pushes to keep us off-balance, an Eytie weapons-carrier gets us in the open. My section hits the dirt, two dead and three wounded. We wriggle back to a dry *wadi* — river bed. Two of our wounded are left out in the open, one with a splintered bloody arm, the other gut-shot. With wounds like that, the best and bravest will sound off in agony.

It's like that for an hour. We snipe at the Italians and they snipe back. We have a Boyes anti-tank rifle set up, but the carrier has slipped away. Not an aircraft in sight, of course, and meanwhile our wounded keep screaming.

Slinger nudges my arm and points to something being flapped on the other side, like a dirty singlet on a rifle. There's an Italian shout: 'Tommi? See the flag? Get your men.'

'Trick?' mutters Slinger.

Maybe. But our guys are still screaming, one calling for his mother — a lot do. I get up and, a moment later, so does an Italian soldier, Bersaglieri Division, their black feather in his hat. He points to my men and stands with hands on hips. He'll stay there until we're done.

Wounded— simple word for real gutted pain. The guy with the shattered arm; it's plastered black with blood and swarming with flies. The gut-wound, his throat is too dry to scream any more; flies across his face, in his nose and open mouth.

The Italian officer stands there all the time, in his neat buff-coloured uniform, that black hat and feather; his boots are brightly polished under their dusting of sand; his face big-nosed with black moustache and a little pointed beard. Dark brown eyes watch me without expression.

A captain, I think. We patch up our men; they patch up theirs. We get the men clear. I turn to the officer.

'Thanks.'

'*Prego*,' he replies.

The wounded men are being carried back. I stay for an awkward moment. He offers me a little brown cigarette, shows me a photo from his wallet. A woman and two kids.

For want of something better, I pull out my wallet and

show him Mum's photo, her and the Virgin Mary. He gives a tight smile, says something in Italian. I nod and smile tightly back. Our blokes are out of sight now so I turn back. So does the black-bearded Bersaglieri officer.

We disengage and pull back. The gut-shot man dies, and we regroup. Creel forms a reinforced patrol and sends us back. It's late afternoon and the Italians are still pushing at our flank; the shadows are dark and the grumble of artillery begins to lessen.

I'm leading the patrol, tense for the sound of half-tracks, so the sudden encounter takes us by surprise. They're at one end of the dry wadi, we're at the other. There are shots, then a short scrambling fight, with bayonets and gun-butts. I knee one man in the groin, gun-butt him over the head. Another crashes into me. I stick the bayonet in and he howls. Hot sticky blood on my hand as I throw him off. Slinger's Thompson gun explodes loud in my ear and it's over.

These troops were Bersaglieri too. The one I gutted with a bayonet is still moaning. It's the black-bearded officer who let us take away our wounded. His eyes roll on me as I kneel beside him, then he gargles, spits blood and is gone. Earlier, he helped save our men. Now my hands are sticky with his blood. But he would have done the same to me. I tell myself that, and scrub my hands with sand to get the blood off them. My hands are shaking and I slap them together, hard.

He would've done the same to me!

'ROBERT, YOU skewered the poor man with a bayonet? What an absolute rotter you are. Surely you know the whole Italian Army is fighting on the wrong side?'

We're in a little Cairo restaurant she's found, eating a lamb curry and dessert with figs and honey. There are no officer uniforms, just Egyptians with their wives or mistresses. Elly looks beautiful in the shadows of red and yellow lanterns. And she's using conversation like bait on a hook. She's fishing and waiting for me to bite. She says I need educating in the wicked ways of the world.

'Do the Eyties know they are on the wrong side?' I ask.

'Of course. Robbie, they were our allies in the last lot.'

'Yes, well so were the Japs,' I say. 'Explain that, Blue-eyes.'

'My eyes are not blue, they are aquamarine. Any-way, the Yanks lit that time-fuse, cutting off all their raw material imports. What should they do, let their economy grind to a stop?'

'Yeah, before then they invaded China.'

'Try some of this sauce, dear, it's delicious. Sesame seed, I think. Yes, they invaded China, well, who hasn't? Such as Britain, Germany, France and Russia. Also the Yanks in the Philippines, the Brits in India and Burma, not to mention Egypt and Ceylon. The French in Indochina, the Dutch, in Indonesia. And ask your Maori friends who invaded New Zealand.'

I choke on a mouthful of curry. Elly gives her wicked little snicker. 'Hah! No answer comes the stern reply!'

I don't give a toss about who invaded where. I do give a toss for this beautiful young woman and her wicked smile. And the hurt in her eyes, that 'no trespass' sign — meaning she still wants to call the shots.

'What about us, Elly — where're we going?'

'Hell in a hand-basket, poppet. Sit back and enjoy the ride.'

'I mean —'

'I know what you mean. Robert, this horrible war won't stop till half of Europe has flattened the other half. Not to mention South-East Asia and the Pacific. Right?'

'Then after that —'

'There is no after. Only a now. Now drink your coffee, we're expected at Angie's houseboat.'

I like what Elly and I have together. I don't want to meet her mates because they are from that different world called Society. The wicked smile is in her eyes, she reads this, out comes her hand over mine.

'You don't want to meet my toffee-nosed mates — no? Gracious as always. You won't, she's in Alexandria, the houseboat's empty.'

'Empty?'

'Yes! Gracious, Robert, do I have to draw you a picture? And do stop spilling your drink — does your mother know you're out?'

Elly is sharp, rude, even insulting, and does not care what she says. That's defence, she spits it out like a tracer. But later that night, we're on the houseboat roof. Searchlights make a shifting pattern over the dark Cairo skies. The steamy muddy smell of the Nile comes in on the night wind.

'The big push will come soon,' says Elly and quivers against me. 'German or British, it will come. And men like you will die, Robbie, so I can't get serious. Do understand.'

I do understand. She was serious once. And later, there's a tear on her cheek as she kisses me goodbye and says, come back soon.

WE GET road-shows and concerts; news films showing our 'gallant wartime girls' on the production line. They're making everything, from bullets to bombers.

Harris says it's a government plot to undermine the unions because women work for lower wages than men. I suggest equal pay and he snaps that would weaken the unions.

Bates is relieved that his blue-eyed Evelyn isn't in some factory. She writes that women like that will 'de-feminise' themselves — and what's wrong with knitting socks and winding bandages?

Sergeants together now, we spend more time together. He even reads out his letter to me. I notice her letters are more about what the Yanks are doing and this young farmer she's met at a dance. She writes what a perfect gentleman he is. Bates is not worried (he knows his Evelyn), so I say nothing.

The American movies are best. Some in the new 'Technicolor' which is so bright it takes some getting used to. Long glossy cars, women in swish outfits and furs, men in smart double-breasted suits and hats. It's another world from this big tent, jammed with unwashed men in dirty uniforms, a big lantern flaring at one end, the big moths zooming around it.

The war movies are best, most in black and white. We can hoot and yell and have a good laugh. The hero always dashes forward in a hail of bullets — try doing that against an M-42 — and every grenade lands bang on target.

The Japs are bucktoothed little guys with spectacles. Never mind that they beat the top British army in Malaya and are giving the Yanks one hell of a fight in the Solomons at Guadalcanal. The Germans are all bull-faced morons who shout '*Sieg Heil!*' before they drop dead. The Italians jabber and run away.

Americans and British are tough-jawed heroes who can fight for a week and stay clean-shaven. I'd like to see them up against the Afrika Korps, or the Ariete, or the Fogliore Division, the latest to prove that Eyties are too damned full of fight.

Harris is critical; wonders why we never see a Russian soldier fighting. They're bloody invisible because (he says) Churchill and Roosevelt want Russia bled white before they invade Europe. He hoots and laughs as the clean-cut heroes win.

And when the show blinks off, we're out into a bitterly cold desert night, the stars overhead like a swish of tiny silver campfires. Shell-fire's grumbling, flares spark up into the sky and the night-bombers drone overhead, because we are taking control of the skies.

We have a cup of lukewarm black tea, thick with sugar, before wrapping ourselves in blankets and shivering to sleep. Tomorrow we'll be fighting bull-faced Krauts and jabbering Eyties, who don't seem to know they're supposed to drop dead when we fire a shot, who think we should drop dead first.

Maybe they've been watching the wrong movies.

Webley service revolver

WE'RE BACK in El Alamein, the sea on one side, the Qattara Depression on the other. Cairo is an easy day's run for the Panzers; all they have to do is bash a hole right through us. A big open car makes lots of dust as it pulls up. We're digging a new gun-pit and trenches because Monty (who Elly says nobody wanted) is in command and setting out a new defensive line.

Anyway, this car pulls up and a little bloke jumps out, strutting towards us. Sharp face and big nose, an old army jersey and tatty cords, Aussie slouch hat tipped to one side — looks like someone's scruffy batman, about to ask directions.

'Got any water, chaps?' A high-pitched voice, British.

'Distilled sea-water, tastes bad,' says Renwick, self-appointed company wit. 'Or chlorine-added, tastes worse.'

The little bloke cackles and looks around. 'Kiwis, eh? I was telling your General Freyberg, you're the finest I have.'

We know who he is now, snap to attention and salute. He just flops a 'stand easy'. A few words about kicking Rommel back to Berlin, then, 'Hey, you chaps got the latest paper?'

The army newspaper. Ernshaw manages to shake his head and Monty flips one over. 'Read mine. Cigarettes?' He throws a pack and Slinger catches it. The car roars off in another cloud of dust.

'Sawed-off little bugger,' mutters Slinger. 'What's the idea of wearing an Aussie hat?'

Ernshaw holds the army paper like it's gold. Given to him by an actual general. Nobody touches this unless with clean hands, no jam-stains or bits ripped off for the latrines. This is going home to his folks as a family keepsake.

Slinger is less reverent about the cigs. I remind them there's a gun-pit to dig. Loudly.

Next day an Aussie despatch-rider drops by, also for water. Pushes up his goggles, tips some over his head and rubs it in. Remarks how the sun's a fair cow and what d'we think of the new little Pommy bastard? All Pom generals are bastards, no reason why this bloke should be any different. Seems nice enough though — for a Pommy bastard.

Turns out Monty stopped at his battalion this morning. Gave them the latest Times, his own copy, even some fags. Reckons Aussies are his best division, just the lads to kick Rommel back to Berlin. Also the little bastard's wearing dinkum Aussie headgear, not one of those lemon-squeezer things Kiwis call a hat.

He roars off in a cloud of dust and insults.

Ernshaw's family keepsake gets cut into pieces for the latrines, the fags are already smoked. Harris mutters something about never trust a Pom, but I grin. At least Montgomery is talking to us, treating us like people — explaining what he wants. But he has to clobber Rommel before Rommel clobbers us. Then he can pull as many strokes as he likes. In fact, we'll even forgive him his bad taste in headgear. In fact, he starts wearing a black tank beret — better.

Now all he has to do is clobber Rommel.

Webley service revolver

CAIRO AND I'M up for the DCM (Distinguished Conduct Medal) over that German tank business. Our Brigadier, Freyberg, is all smiles as he pins it on me, and Creel pumps my hand. I have leave, he says, get lost for forty-eight hours.

So, next stop the hostel and Elly. Lady Epsom Salts gives me a look that would curdle milk. Elly greets me with a loud squawk of delight. She knows all the back-alley bars and leads me to one. Of course, she is doing all the talking.

'Robbie, another gong? You'll get yourself killed.'

'Tell that to the Panzer that was trying to squash me.'

'Rubbish, the poor guy was just lost and wanted directions home.'

'Why the hell do I bother with you, Elly?'

'Because I'm adorable, poppet. Oh look, there's Eddie Brougham, complete with silver nut.'

'What?'

'Sherwood Foresters, darling. Silver Acorn badge, as in oak trees, as in Sherwood Forest. You know — Robin Hood and his Merry Men?'

'Is he a boyfriend?'

'Robin Hood? Oh, you mean Eddie, now don't be jealous, poppet, doesn't become you. The only chap I'm keen on is the sun-bronzed Kiwi non-com, recently decorated.'

'Who … oh?'

'I love the way you spill your beer, darling. And remember what I said about killing yourself. Uncle Joe and the Yanks are the only winners in the war. I mean, what's your little New Zealand getting out of it?'

'Dunno. Well, we're stopping a dictator —'

'What do you think Joe Stalin is, a choir-boy?'

'All right then, we're fighting so there won't be another war.'

'The war to end all wars? They used that excuse last time, poppet. And shouldn't you be back, defending hearth and home?'

'You're a stirrer, you know that.'

'And loving it, poppet. Oh, look, Gervase St Clair,

Scots Guards. Smile, darling, wave, show your teeth. Another lecture about consorting with the lower classes coming up tomorrow, I expect. One girl got bunged off to Kenya. Mind you, she was going out with a Canadian — oh, laugh, Robert. That was a joke!'

'I don't know what to make of your jokes.'

'No, darling, because you're always brooding. You didn't have a father, so accept that. Acting like him won't help.'

'I don't act like him. Hell, Elly, don't say that — *not that!*'

'You do, Robert. All these heroics, just like him? Proving yourself better? You'll get killed doing that. Oh, write to your mother, she probably feels to blame for everything.'

'Why the hell should she?'

'She couldn't keep her hero-husband in the home; oh that had to be her fault, not his. D'you think she wants you coming back a war hero — like him?'

'Mind your own business.'

'Rather thought I was.'

And I just do not understand her. One minute her smile is wicked and dancing; next there's a deep frightened look. Elly's beautiful here in the stink of oil-lamps. She has on a crimson-red dress, just off the colour of blood. Her black hair shines. There's the clink of glasses, her deep voice and her sometimes loud laughter. She sips her drink — orange juice.

'Robbie,' she takes another sip and puts the glass down carefully. 'It's a shame you never talked to him.'

'Maybe he never gave me the chance. Elly, I don't want to spend this leave talking about him.'

She's suddenly wicked and dancing again. 'So let's talk about where we're sleeping tonight. Oh, did I say that rather loudly? Did people hear, do you think?'

'Just about all Cairo, you awful Pommy sheila. That's right, laugh.'

We finish our drinks. Hell, Elly is so close and so distant. She pulls me in and pushes me out. She's some class-miles above me, but like me. Out of place and out of time.

We leave the bar. Elly (of course) has somewhere for us to go. We should spend it in lovemaking but this night, she just cries. For me, I think, not her. But just holding her close is okay too. Thinking about Jacko.

Shame I never talked to him!

SURE, ELLY, and should my mum feel guilty about the little rental houses we grew up in, bare floors and no coal for the fire? Ragged dirty blankets, just bread-and-dripping to eat. Mum spending a lot of time telling her rosary. Spending more time at her cleaning job.

Aunt Francesca was married to a farmer. She'd visit with food and cast-offs, playing Lady Bountiful. One birthday she brought me some soldiers, lead ones in khaki and tin helmets, running with their rifle and bayonet presented. Chargers, they were called — twelve, complete with officer and sword.

I loved those soldiers. Lined them up and fought battles; their enemies were clothes-pegs or marbles. They had night actions by the light of a candle-stump. They were my soldiers and always won their battles.

One Saturday we were going to the movies. That was very special, and the night before, I was too excited to sleep, so I lit the candle-stump for a night-battle. I fell asleep and that night my father made one of his visits.

I woke to shouting and someone bumping unsteadily against the corridor, then against my door, lurching in as it flew open, letting light into the room.

My father was there, leaning against the door. I could smell the stench of beer, hear his wheezy breath as he took one unsteady step in.

My mother's frightened face looked at me over his shoulder. 'Oh, Robert, you should be in bed.'

My father, lurching another step forward, looked down. 'Boy's playing soldiers?'

I was scared. The times my dad was home, I often got a hiding. So I scrambled up, waiting for those big hands to move to his belt. He's still looking down at the line of soldiers, nudges one with his shoe. A battered shoe, open at the toe. The soldier is knocked over, topples others over too.

'Fallen over, eh … dead?' He wheezes again.

I'm up against the bed, shaking, waiting for the belt to come off. Mum's huddled at the door, hand to mouth. He nudges his shoe again and they all fall, except for the officer. He reaches unsteadily down and picks it up. Even presses his finger against the sword.

'Officer … saving his skin … didn't finish the job.'

Then suddenly he stamps his foot down hard on the tumbled line, again and again, crushing them into flattened lumps of lead. Stamping and stamping, then with a queer whimper of pain he dropped to his knees.

He was still holding the officer-figure, looking at it. 'Should've done for you ... yellow bastard ... yellow —' and crumpling it in his fist. A trickle of blood where the sword stabbed him. Dropping it, now on his hands and knees, then over to one side. A loud ragged snoring sound.

Mum took me into the hall. She slipped a pillow under his head, covered him with my blankets. I slept on the couch and in the morning he was gone.

We didn't go to the movies. I think she gave him the money. Aunt Francesca got me more soldiers but I never played with them. I was afraid he'd come back so I swapped them for marbles — 'steelies', solid metal; he couldn't crush those.

He didn't come back. It was the last time I saw him — until the hospital.

I HAD ONE more day of leave left. Elly and I would be spending it together. I went to pick her up, but she wasn't there.

A week later, I still had the bruises.

I waited outside the hotel. The plaster was still flaking off those horrible statues. No sign of Elly so I wandered into the foyer. And there's Epsom Salts walking up with a thin smile on her face.

'Oh, sergeant ...' she says the word like 'maggot' or 'scab', and there's something not-nice about that arch smile. She points down the corridor, 'Try the room at the end.'

She's off with a starchy swish of petticoats, so I shrug and go down, knock on the end door and enter. It's shut at once behind me. It's a small room with brooms, cleaning stuff and a door leading to a side-exit. An officer's sitting on the edge of a table — British, playing with one of those 'swagger sticks' they all carry; red staff tabs and a fancy regiment badge; a long fair moustache, his cap pulled over his eyes.

'Ah …' His cap's so far down he has to raise his face to see me. I know his type and I've seen that look before. Everyone's a bloody peasant, old chap. 'You Moran?'

I nod. Aware that the two blokes who closed the door are big non-coms from the same regiment. He plays with the swagger stick a moment and shakes his head slightly. 'It really won't do, old chap. You and Elly. Simply not on. Mater's in a dreadful tiz.'

So this is the brother … 'Where is Elly?' I ask.

He tilts his cap back, and lifts an eyebrow, looks very polite and blank, gently taps his swagger stick against one polished boot. 'Who knows? On her way to India, Simla, I think. Damn good polo this time of the year.'

She'd been posted? 'She never said anything to me. Can I write to her?'

'Rather you didn't.' Tap-tap goes the stick against his boot. 'Our Elly's a bit of a tease, you know. Bit of a flirt. Likes her boyfriends rough.'

'I'll bloody write to her if I want to.'

'Rather hoping you wouldn't take that line, old chap.' The swagger stick motions up the non-coms. 'Explain to him, will you, lads?'

'Closing ranks,' Elly called it. I should have been expecting this. The non-coms grab me. The officer is back to tapping his boots as they hustle me outside, into a little courtyard, piled with boxes, quite dark. Up a narrow arched alley, the noise and lights of Cairo come loudly. I'm pushed through the door and fall to the stinking flagstones, clammy with mud. I try to get up and a boot thuds painfully into my ribs, another into my side.

'Got the message, thicko?' says one non-com.

'Get stuffed —' and another boot hits me in the face.

'You need to learn the hard way,' mutters one.

'Look on the bright side,' grunts the other. 'A few cushy weeks in hospital.'

They are taking off their berets, tucking them into their pockets. They drag me up and slam me against the wall. The first punch comes hard in my ribs, the second in my stomach. My knees are buckling already. When I'm on the ground, the boots will go back to work.

'Oi, cobber!' comes another voice. 'Not so much racket, eh?'

The non-coms turn. A dark shape is squatting in the far corner, almost lost in the shadows. Moonlight glints off a bottle as he stands, stepping into the lights — a thickset Australian, slouch hat over to one side.

'That's not an Aussie you're fooling round with, is it?'

One non-com growls. 'Sod off, you mucking colonial no-hoper, or you'll get the same as your Kiwi mate.'

The Aussie rocks on his heels a moment. 'Listen you …' His voice comes very slow and drawling. 'No-hoper' and 'colonial' I can take. But implying I've got a Kiwi mate … Hear that, Snow?'

'Flaming right I did, Ernie.'

A second dark shadow, even more thickset, stands.

Another bottle glints, there's a glugging swallow and the bottle drops with a smash. 'Snow' has a hard, battered face. He wipes his mouth.

'Wouldn't let a Kiwi clean my boots,' he grumbles. 'Mind you, I wouldn't piss on a Pom.'

Two Brits against two Aussies, so the result is a foregone conclusion. Ernie punches one. Snow punches the other. Then, in a nice bit of teamwork, they smack their heads together. Both the non-coms go down against the wall.

'Bloody cheeky buggers, man can't even have a quiet drink,' says Ernie. He looks at me. 'Rack off, you.'

They've saved me from a really bad beating. 'What about a drink together?'

Ernie shakes his head very sadly. 'Drink with a Kiwi? Social ruin, mate, social ruin. We'd never live it down.'

'I'm buying.'

'That's different. Lead on, cobber.'

They explain that out-drinking Kiwis is part of their basic training — and I spend my last Gippo pound proving them right. Snow assures me I'll never make a dinkum Queenslander but he's known worse Tasmanians. I think that's a compliment.

We part company at my hotel. There's a pain in my ribs, a big bruise under one eye. And another pain from thinking about Elly. Her 'establishment' has closed ranks. Somewhere else I do not belong.

I did make inquiries. One of her friends said she'd try and get her address. She also warned me to keep away from the hostel. It might be a knife in the ribs next time. And she wasn't joking.

She did get the address and I did write. No answer. After the war, I find the mail-ship was torpedoed. But I can't forget those wicked eyes and that bright smile. And what she said about the secret war, that we knew nothing about.

MAYBE THERE'S no room for love in war. I wonder if old Jacko learned that lesson too. And I know that Elly and me in peacetime wouldn't work either.

So — then — it was back to the lines at El Alamein and wondering if Rommel would beat Monty to the punch. His Panzers were only a couple of hours from Cairo then.

El Alamein, 1942

FRIDAY, 23 OCTOBER, 9.15 p.m. The cold desert night cuts into my bones. A thin wind lifts the gritty sand onto my face, scraping oddly along the sides of the Bren-carrier beside me. Her armour-plate is like ice. Unseen men shuffle and fidget around me; the stink of their perspiration is not frozen. Beside me, Ernshaw coughs, clears his throat.

'Geeze, it's sodding cold. What time is it, sarge?'

'Ernshaw, you asked me that a minute ago. Shut up.'

'Hey, Robbie, what odds it'll be cancelled again?'

'Shut up, Slinger.'

'I vote we don't move until the bloody tanks do.'

'Shut up, Harris. Next bloke that opens his mouth gets my boot in it.'

All of this in savage whispers. Thousands of blokes like us are waiting in the cold, utter blackness, waiting the last ten minutes. Because this is the night, and we will attack.

I could die or have bits of me — chunks of me, shot away. I've seen it happen. Blink — just like that. Blink, your arm's shattered, your face shot away. Blink — your guts are a bloody mess. Blink — you're dead.

Creel is walking down the line, stops beside me, even manages to sound excited. 'Few minutes, sergeant. The

145

Trojans built their fires in the plain and stood to arms all night.'

He's off. No fires, just some flares going up, some artillery, to make it all sound normal. The big Sherman tanks loom black ahead with their exhaust stink and engine-noise — because they have to rev up at intervals or freeze.

The Jerries must hear! Chrissake, can't they sense what I do? Just our sweat and tension alone must be rolling into them like a thick cloud. I have the Bren, a bandolier of spare clips, Ernshaw has more. Some hard tack, a full canteen of cold tea. I strike a match quickly, blow it out.

9.20 p.m. Five minutes to go. Minefields ahead in the blackness. We have routes through, 'navigation' officers to lead us. Ours, a fresh Second-Lieutenant Daly, has got sod's own chance and knows it.

I think about Elly and that last night; even about the letter I posted home to Mum today. The usual crap about things being okay. Blink. If I die, she'll get the telegram before the letter. Should have put a hell of a lot more into that letter but there's too much distance. Might as well write to my father.

It will start any minute now!

Sorry you died in that hospital, Dad. Peacetime killed you. I know about war now, and sodding heroics. You waited your time like this at Gallipoli and Flanders — for the signal to get up and die.

Creel's beside me, close, his breath stinking of

peppermints. 'Sergeant. Balloon's going up any moment. Keep low, keep behind the tanks and keep moving. Good luck.'

Our helmet rims scrape as I nod. He's moving on. Balloon going up? Meaning a Jerry mine might rip me apart? Slamming bullets make my last movement the untidy twirl-about of death? That bloke at Mingar Qaim, holding one torn-off arm in the other hand. Blink.

It will happen. Blink!

And the ground shudders to a crashing monster wave-beat of destruction. Artillery, some nine hundred guns open up along the front line. A roaring tempest of flashing yellow flame and screaming shells, like hell unchained. A hissing popping flarelight, white and glaring like the colour of cold hell.

Get moving!

In that nightmare, deafening moment, shouting, everyone's shouting. I'm staggering like I'm caught in a storm-blast. The shellfire thundering. Concussing. Engine-growl and hot exhaust fumes as the tank ahead lurches and grinds forward. And adding to the din, a second orchestra of deadly red tracer as the Germans return our fire. Their own artillery open up.

We are running — staggering and wading — into this black din of screaming, exploding shells and the first screams of hurt men, because Jerry has our range to the yard. Cannot stop, yelling at the men to keep moving — *keep moving!* Follow the shrill peal of our officers' whistles.

Ahead, our tank shudders to a dusky red explosion. The armour-plated beast lurches, wounded, a thick gout of flame bursts through the turret hatch, flickering sharp and red on my cheeks as I run past; mercifully no screams from inside.

Inside this screaming, thundering blackness now. The earth shaking, the black night flashing red fires, full of screaming thunder. And the noise rises and rises. To our left another tank explodes — don't think about it — *move!*

So, into the night, split with the dark colours of thunder and death. Run, ducking your head against the sleeting metal storm, the screaming splinters of death and the ground shaking. Going on — *on!*

A weapon-pit ahead, we are yelling and screaming, Creel in front as we tumble over the sandbags and fight the gunners. Slinger jabs his bayonet into one, the man screams. Ernshaw, glaring and teeth clenched, clubs another.

'On — *on!*' shouts Creel, waving his revolver.

On into a black hell of thunder, smoke and hell-colours. I trip on young Daly's shattered body — *someone will write to his folks* — stagger into the shell-blasted black hell and pray that death stays that blink away.

Blink —

We scatter to the whiplash of bullets. Dawn now, white and green flares still stud the half-lit sky, showing black smoke and yellow fire, and tanks everywhere — burning, shattered, or just leaning over like stupid dead things.

Ahead of us, a Honey takes a sideways hit. From a Jerry anti-tank Pak-45mm, dug in somewhere close. The commander collapses over his turret, binoculars in one hand. They shatter on the armour-plate. One crewman gets out, the gunner, flinching against bullets rattling the armour-plate. He lands heavily on the ditch, runty and brown-haired; one side of his face is a massive swollen bruise. I pull him down. The tank settles and does not catch on fire. Excellent cover.

Another 45mm shell glances off the Honey, making it settle further. There's a thick smell of diesel fuel and choking black smoke as another Honey burns. We're pinned down, Creel nowhere in sight.

Ernshaw crawls up, his face smudged with oil. 'Got that Pak spotted, sarge. On the rise, thirty yards —'

Tak-tak-tak-tak. And Ernshaw is flung wriggling over, helmet torn off, beating his heels on the ground. I pull him under cover and he screams, gut-shot, and the bright blood jets high. Almost a comical dismay on his oil-smeared face.

'Gee, sarge, am I stuffed, is it bad?'

'No way, son, easy patch-up. Lie still, okay.'

'Sarge, my guts are on fire. Geeze, I'm bloody bleeding —'

'Hang on, son —' *son, he's my age!* 'I'll slap a dressing on, lie still, the doc'll patch you up —' I'm trying to think of Ernshaw's first name, can't.

He's pale under the sand, oil and desert tan. Slinger's crawled up, gives a shocked look, and hands over the dressing. Oh hell, those tumbling guts everywhere.

I grab a fluttering hand. Somehow the battle fades like turning down a knob on a radio. Ernshaw is whispering, gasping.

'Not fair, it's not fair, sarge. Shit, I'm —'

His eyes are still open but blank, sand settling on his eyelashes. His fingers are limp as weeds and I let go. Fair? When you're nineteen you think you'll live forever.

'He's gone, mate, sorry,' says the runty little brown-haired tank driver. Slinger spits, tips Ernshaw's helmet over his face. The full battle-din is storming around us again like a switch is turned on. The runty driver speaks again, nervous. 'Maybe we should pull back, sitting ducks here.'

I sit up, my helmet bangs against the side of the tank. *Not fair!* That hot and cold tingle, wanting to yell, tears prickle my eyes like they're gritty with sand. *Not fair!*

The rage is flooding me, dreamlike and cold, click-click as I load another clip on the Bren. Another 45mm shell screams over, light enough to see the scramble of dark figures on either side, the black untidy wreckage of battle. I'm thinking, cold. Harris is up now, too.

'You.' I grab the runty gunner. 'Get on that tank machine-gun. I want covering fire.' He doesn't want to but sees the look in my eyes. 'Slinger, here, covering fire.'

Harris makes to open his mouth, shuts it. The rage is still flooding me like a cold river. If that Pak gunner can see us, we can see him. Thirty yards on the rise, Ernshaw said — Malcolm, yes, that's his first name.

I can see it now, nicely dug in, long-barrelled, a gun-shield. The tac-tac-tac of the machine-gun, Slinger and

Harris working their rifles. I'm crawling forward, stones cutting my elbows and knees, pushing the Bren before me, pulling a grenade out. The gunners will see the tank still firing. Okay, slam another round into it. The barrel is moving a little so I flip the pin on one grenade and throw. I stand up as I do and run, throw another. Two explosions, enough to make them duck.

And yes — I can see the crouching gunners. I kneel, steady the Bren. Tac-tac-tac-tac. Close enough to see my bullets bouncing off the gunshield. Click on another round, walking forward. Bullets zip around me, an explosion chucks dirt into my face. I'm firing now into the shield slit, the barrel jerks but does not fire again.

A last grenade, then I'm scrambling over into the gun-pit, in the smoke of its explosion. Three crew huddle around the gun-breech. In another scramble, Harris and Slinger join me. The runty little gunner has wisely stayed behind. Slinger drops down, tipping his helmet back. He's already eyeing an Iron Cross one of those Jerries is wearing. 'You're a mad bugger, Moran, you know that.'

'Bloody mad,' mutters Harris, 'considering the pittance we get.'

We seem to have made a dent in the German line here. Some more of our blokes appear, Creel with them. He whistles, shakes his head. But we have to regroup, keep moving. We've given the Germans one hell of a kick but they're not beaten.

Not by a long shot.

The full day blurs into another night. Then more like them — days and nights of howling destruction. We're sand-grimed, half our section down. I've got a bashed shoulder, I swear a cracked rib. All of us are wounded. Creel has a charmed life.

He's ahead all the time, shouting, organising. We follow and it's so good to be moving ahead. To see burning German tanks now, shattered German weapon pits, even their evil 88mm guns bombed into scrap iron. Our airforce has the skies — Hurricanes, Tomahawks, fighters and bombers blasting a way ahead.

And it's good to be moving, pushing and, this once, with the Afrika Korps on the back foot. Monty's whole machine is cracking their lines, dive-bombing through their minefields. Harvey is dead, Suger, Bowcock, and Raynor. Conway stepped on a Bouncing Betty. He's alive but forget that tribe of kids he was always talking about. Forget walking without crutches.

Tilly died in Greece. Hell, I'd stopped thinking about him.

We're moving faster than our supply columns. Living off German sausage, black bread and their bitter acorn coffee.

One tragic moment with Slinger. Three weeks into the fighting, I notice he's staggering. Then that he's lumping a big haversack. Creel has noticed it too and orders Slinger to empty it.

Out come Lugers, Iron Crosses, Knights Crosses, the fancy diamonds and oak-leaf clusters. Cigarette cases, signet-rings, a whole tangle of wristwatches. Metal clasp-knives, a tight wad of German money, even gold coins, silver religious medallions.

Creel kicks the whole lot aside and stamps through them. He tells Slinger that if he puts just one medal back into his haversack then he — Creel — will shoot him. He says Slinger is the biggest thief in the whole Eighth Army.

Slinger looks so injured and even downcast that Creel relents; lets him keep a few Knights Crosses.

Yes, Slinger's easily the biggest thief in the whole Eighth Army. I sometimes think he is also the best actor.

British PIAT gun

'THEY TRIED TO con me into tanks,' mutters Slinger. 'Not for quids.'

I know what he means. We just knocked out a Panzer. Ours or theirs, tankers die hard. When a tank is hit, they have just over a minute, tops, to get out — or burn alive. This Panzer crew does not get out; they howl and scream for too long. Black smoke covers their tank, then comes the red flame.

Our tanks are up; we are secure this night. We eat bully beef, hard army biscuits and sip hot sweet tea. The flames of the burning tank beat upon our faces.

I don't think much about my family. I write letters to Mum sometimes, not to my younger brother and sister. They wrote to me — once. Hell, what do I write about?

Being halfway through the Alamein offensive, stinking and dog-tired? The battlefield stench of decay, the bodies black with the heat and swollen by gases? The awful tense knotted fear?

Creel comes up, his face pale under a three-day stubble, his voice croaking, slips beside me, mutters something about 'dogs of war' — another quote I think — and gulps from my canteen. Sighs.

'Ajax, Achilles, Hector — they would have raised their swords. I can just see you in the triple-crested helmet and clashing bronze.' His face is sticky from sweat and sand, his voice high-pitched because he's on the edge. We all are. 'Got a letter from the Mater. She and Father divorced, know that?' No, I do not and I don't want to. I just want to sleep — get that burning stench out of my nose. Creel is still talking, bone-tired like me. 'Anyway she tells me something about your dad and my dad, crap, I mean she was the one caught in bed with —'

He breaks off. I think because he has said too much. No, he's just asleep, helmet tilted over his face. So I push myself up and check the sentries, smell the charred horrible stench from that burning tank.

In the morning, we are ready to move, our artillery already screaming overhead and pounding the German lines. Creel has shaved, is as pink-cheeked as ever and bright as hell. He moves among us, checking equipment and ammo, making jokes. Smoke from the burning tank still drifts in the pale morning air. He makes no mention of last night.

More troops are coming up and our Shermans are

clanking behind them. Each has a sand-goggled officer in the hatch. One looks over at that burned-out Panzer — and looks away. I don't blame him. The tank is black, the barrel twisted. Puddles of fat congeal underneath, from the bodies of the crew, a black greedy buzz of flies over them. Through the torn hull are their carbonised remains, shrunk to the size of big black dolls.

I won't write home about that, either.

AFTER MORE than a full month of fighting, we're sleep-walking. I am shaking, filthy and stinking. I am screaming for sleep, have forgotten about good food and water. And life is just the next rise, or entrenched weapons pit. Or slit-ted eyes straining into the dust clouds for a Panzer, watching the sky for a German strike, watching the ground for a mine.

The Afrika Korps are still retreating but resisting, stubborn, using every fold of ground, their bloody good guns blasting away at us. From ahead comes the scream-ing whip-crack of another 88mm gun.

We have no tanks behind us. Our last Honey went over a Teller mine, a thing about the size of a dustbin-lid, and is brewing up behind us. 'Brewing up' means it's on fire — but at least the trapped crew have stopped scream-ing. Honeys can't tackle an 88mm. Just about nothing can.

Creel kneels beside me, lips cracked, his face caked white with dust, helmet dented from a near miss and a field-dressing around his arm. He's grinning though — as always — and I expect an *Iliad* quote to come spouting from his lips. 'Take it in flank,' he whispers hoarsely. 'Work your section around the side, take enough grenades, they'll have machine-guns. Grenades, you'll need a lot.'

He is a damned good soldier. Too good to make mistakes, but the best of us do. When we are bone-tired, aching and dead from lack of sleep, caked with dust and dinned with concussion. Creel gets up on one knee to look back —

'Geddown!' I shout.

There's another loud 88mm whip-crack as Creel turns. Something slams into me and I'm flung down, my tin helmet digging into the dirt. Something thumps on top of me. I roll over, stunned, dirty and spitting earth. I see Creel.

His blue eyes are open and looking at me. His mouth's open and he's still moving but only slightly. The top half of him's moving, sliding on blobby red ribbons — the rest of him back somewhere, thrown wherever that last 88mm shell cut him at the waist and went on without exploding.

Blink! Cut him in half! Those blobby red ribbons are his intestines!

I want to choke, vomit, like that Jerry shell slammed into my guts too. But he is dead — blink — so, push it away — *wrench it away!* — because the damned 88mm is still out there.

Slinger is crawling up, gapes as he sees that half-Creel. I kick him and shout to get moving. We have an 88mm to take out, that will mean calling in an air-strike. We have things to do so must leave that Creel-thing behind and I must swallow my gagging vomit. Creel's revolver

156

somehow in my hand, I wave it — get moving — get moving!

We have a gun to take out. I push Creel away from my mind, like Tilly, go on — and on.

NIGHT. ANOTHER endless night of crump-crump artillery, white and yellow flares dimming the moonlight, that awful spitting red tracer. Low-flying Tomahawks shot out the 88mm with their rockets. We are okay for tonight but the thunder of battle is all around us.

Slinger comes up, offers his canteen. I'm expecting vintage brandy but get cold tea. Good enough, I drink more than I should. We're in another weapons pit, eating bully beef from a can, and the bone-aching exhaustion makes everything glassy and slow-moving.

'Creel,' says Slinger, 'he was all right.'

I have to force the spoonful of bully into my mouth. I have to chew and nod. He was all right. Damned good and now damned gone; me, a veteran (so-called) but still coming awake to all this.

Blink.

Yes, Slinger, and they'll send someone else; and we will go on to the next Afrika Korps defence line. And our new captain will lead us on — maybe get himself shot into bloody strings. So, the awful things go on — so, like Tilly, Creel is pushed from my mind.

We have to go on.

IT'S LIKE A punch, like a huge fist slamming into me, knocking me sideways somehow, knock-kneed at the same time, spinning me around. The Bren's flung away, the ground slams up hard to smack me in the face. I'm rolling over, one side of my body numb, somehow my right arm's underneath. There's an odd noise — me, gasping and moaning, like I'm winded.

And somehow the shellfire is tuned down and distant. I'm beside some sandbags, I can see every detail; the sand trickling out from holes made by shell-fragments. Slinger's on his knees beside me, looking gob-smacked, yelling for First-Aid. I can feel something now. It starts like a dull thudding, then kicks into a pounding fire of pain. I hear a new sound, gasping and high-pitched — I'm trying to move my body to be more comfortable — realise I am gasping in pain and writhing in agony. Blood's warm and sticky all over me — *gut-shot like Ernshaw!*

Slinger's holding me, saying something, crooning like I'm a kid. Bates is up with First Aid, a jab in my arm. And those raw jagged flames of agony are softening as the morphine takes hold. They're bundled into a blanket, Harris cursing at the blokes to be careful. Slinger promises a slap-up Cairo meal, a whole crate of beer if I'll just be a sensible bastard and pull through.

Blink.

The Aid station. Tent walls shaking in the blast of shellfire, big yellow lanterns surrounded by clouds of moths, screams and howls around me, the sharp tang of antiseptic, the warm stink of blood, flies buzzing greedily. A white-faced, unshaven doctor looks at me, writes something on my forehead, another jab —

Blink.

The ambulance goes as slow as it can but bumps and jars on the rutted roads. The man in the bunk down from mine is screaming and calling for his mother. Water's coming in from somewhere and dripping on my face — odd, thick, warm-tasting water. It's blood from the stretcher in the rack above; an arm dangles down, nice wristwatch. Slinger would have that.

And the pain's growing … A medic checks my forehead mark, no more painkiller, had too much. I still hear screaming but it's me, my body wrenched with that red-hot pain … drifting into wobbly darkness but the sharp pain always there, my throat cracked with screaming —

Blink.

A white dazzling light overhead, a man in white, stained with blood. Masked man, white mask, careful tired eyes. Voice speaking, wound to small intestine, liver damage, arm broken. Loss of blood, shock. Hold tight, son, have to operate now. The sweetish sickly fumes of chloroform, hold tight, what the hell does that mean? Drifting now into a better black darkness, bottomless and sinking.

White again. A white ceiling, white sheets and white-uniformed nurses. All spotlessly white. They say you can't feel pain in two places at once. But my arm pounds like someone's stamping a sharp boot on it. My body feels like it's being sandpapered with fire.

I'm sweating, a nurse dabs my forehead with something cool. Says I have to lie still and sleep. I ask about my mates, the battalion, she just shakes her head. Battle's still rolling full blast, no word. I must lie back and sleep.

My broken arm will take some weeks to set. My stomach is ripped its length by a shell fragment. The surgeon, one of those jovial red-faced, grey-whiskered guys, tells me any lower and I'd have lost something they couldn't stitch back on again. Ha, bloody ha.

I'm out of the war for three months. And it's bloody crazy that I should feel guilty. That my mates are copping it while they crack the Afrika Korps. Because the New Zealand Division is used like a sledge-hammer. And we have the full hospital wards and all those rough graves with rifles stuck on them, to prove it.

And Monty, that little bantam-bloke in the baggy trousers and old army sweater, has pulled it off. The greatest victory of the war to date. He has cracked Rommel's best troops and bundled them back. Rommel's Panzer fleets are burned-out scrap iron in the desert. His airforce shot out of the skies. There's plenty of fight left in the Afrika Korps. But they are on the run and will stay that way.

Bates comes to see me with a bag of oranges. He says the Vitamin C will be good for me. That he's written to the scout troop, telling them how I took on that Pak-45mm gun. I hope I never run into them after the war.

There's a new company captain, Shaw. Good enough but the boys miss Creel (says Bates). Yes, I miss him too, even that *Iliad* stuff. He saved us on Crete. And he's gone. This war has a long way to run, odds on chance I'll join him.

Slinger comes too. He says a smart guy would've got

a leg-wound, be shipped home for a cert then. But (he says with a cheerful evil grin) when I recover, I'm going back up the line. Meanwhile do I need anything — for a price of course.

And that slap-up Cairo meal and the crate of beer he promised?

Slinger gives me an offended look. That was a low blow. Reminding a chap of a few hasty words in the middle of battle — when the chap in question was saving the other chap's life. Slinger made it sound like he'd personally arranged a truce with Rommel to get me out. He's disgusted at my ingratitude. Sure he'll run to a beer and sandwiches at an army canteen. Besides, I had a gut-wound and rich food might kill me. He'd never forgive himself. He's got a bar of chocolate for me, that's all I can expect right now. He marches off with a big wave. I'm so pleased to see him, I nearly forget to be rude.

Bren gun

THERE WERE BIG cemeteries in Egypt. Well, we did leave some thousands there. I was nearly one of them.

I was on light duties at HQ, Cairo when I came out of hospital, and Captain Watkins pulled me aside.

Am I all right to drive now? I nod, which is a mistake because I get a job I won't like.

The graves aren't much to look at. Wooden crosses leaning sideways in the loose Cairo sand. An upturned helmet, the bowl eaten out by rust. So Old Man Creel leans on his stick and watches with his pale blue eyes. He's a politician, here on some fact-finding thing. Here also to see his son's grave. And Watkins gave me the duty. 'Don't drive him into a minefield, please.'

The sarky bugger; 'please' is like a four-letter word. So I had saluted and gone to get a jeep. And driven Old Creel out to where we'd buried his son — all we could find of him.

At last, Creel clears his throat and turns. 'I understand that all graves will be in a proper war cemetery. My wife and I think it proper that Richard should lie there. Corner of a foreign field, eh? Remember the poem?'

No, I don't, but he seems to. There are tears in his eyes now and one trickles down his chubby pink cheek. He's fumbling with a little Box Brownie, manages to take a picture. Then another. He puts the camera carefully back into its leather case.

'Thank you, er …' a glance at my sleeve, 'sergeant. What did you say your name was?'

'Moran, sir.'

The door's open, he's about to get back into the jeep. Then he stops and turns. There's a glint in his eyes like — fear? Calculation? A curious look, like he's forgotten about his son and the war. He cocks his head like a bird.

'Moran? Oh yes. Silly of me not to register.' And he's twirling his cane, slitting his pale blue eyes like a shrewd old rooster.

'Jacko Moran was my father, sir.'

He blinks like I hit him. Then those blue eyes go crinkly, the tears are back. His fat pink face seems to sag. For about a minute it's like that, his body shaking. 'I served with your father, Sergeant Moran. Did he tell you about me?'

'Never really knew him, sir. Never told me nothing.'

Him and my dad — something happened. Creel is fearful, round-shouldered and somehow shrinking back.

'He told you nothing. Nothing?'

'No, sir —'

'Ah.' He nods. 'Good man, always ready for a fight. There when I got my wound.' He laughs bitterly. 'Your dad would know about wounds. And letters.'

'Letters, sir?'

He has one foot inside the jeep, leaning on his cane. The river is muddy brown, the sun stinking hot and the black flies whirl like tiny Stukas. Every bright bead of sweat is a target.

'Yes, letters, about how death was instant and with-out pain; I got one of those. How the boy was beloved of the battalion. Those letters.'

For a moment, I don't click. His son was okay, we did like him. And it was painless, has to be when an 88mm shell cuts you in half. What did he think we'd write about — the blood? The poor bugger's guts? And he's seen this in my eyes, maybe thinks I am covering the truth, scrambles into the jeep like he's escaping. I get into the driver's seat, slam the door. Look at him.

'Ah … Mr Creel, it was painless —'

He says nothing. I get him back to Base, he transfers to a car and is driven off. I slap the flies and dust from my face. He hasn't said a word. What was the old bugger on about? That his boy really died in screaming agony and we're not telling him? Hell, I was telling the truth!

Slinger supplies the answer that night. He hands me a hot cup of black sweet tea. 'He's a politician, mate. They're so full of crap that they naturally assume everyone else is.' He slurps his tea noisily. 'The old bugger's been chasing votes too long.'

Maybe. Even then, I thought there was something else. Something I didn't know.

I never saw Old Creel again. About a day later, though, Watkins told me he suffered some kind of turn in Cairo. That he'd been shipped home. I felt really bad when I heard that.

Hell, I was telling the truth!

Webley service revolver

Korea, 1951

IT'S RAINING. *Thick warm drops that come crashing down in vertical lines and drench everything. It's been raining for about six weeks and will rain for some six weeks more. Monsoon weather and everything is damned wet. And muddy.*

The war has bogged down in mud. Worse mud than North Africa and Italy, if that's possible. And the rain is drumming on our tent like we're under a giant shower-bath. Everything is damp, the ground is wet. Every damned fly in Korea is taking shelter in our tent.

We are pulled back. Even the war has ground to a halt in this mud; rather, bogged down. The battle-lines have stabilised more or less where the old boundary was between North and South Korea. And in a place called Panmunjon, they are talking armistice. Cease-fire.

Sometime in the future, snaps Shank, just in from the rain, chucking off his oilskins. First things first, though; important things like the length of the flagpoles, the shape of the tables and who enters the conference room first.

And we're still being told that the Chinese and North Koreans are on the ropes. Problem is, they don't seem to know it.

Ask the Yanks at Pork Chop Hill, or Snipers Ridge. Or the Brits at the Hook. A dozen other strong points, all attacked hard. We've fired so many shells that the barrels of our Twenty-four Pounders are just about melted off.

I'M TRYING *to write a letter home, but my pen just digs out lumps of damp paper. The ink smears and runs. I screw it into a ball and pitch it out into the rain, watch it float away.*

Across the way, a Korean family are trying to haul their ox out of the mud, mired up to its knees — There's a white-bearded old man in a long smock and funny little black hat, two women with their heads wrapped in scarves, a little boy in an outsize ragged T-shirt. They pull hard because oxen are life for peasants. It's sinking deeper though, the low mooing of distress comes clearly to us. One of the women clutches her head and wails.

This war has got to end. Yeah, and I said that about the last one.

Bren gun

May, 1943

IT DID COME to an end in North Africa. It took a hundred thousand Yanks coming in one direction and our Eighth Army from the other. But we did push the Afrika Korps into Tunisia.

I came back in on the very end. I saw those desert wild-flowers in spring, colour after colour, red, yellow, purple and blue, splashing themselves over the fields — between the ugly blotches of brown shell-craters, where the Afrika Korps had fought every step of the way.

They put up this Mesah line and Monty needs his best outfit again — us. We attacked, first into a blinding locust storm, the insects splattering into yellow mulch against us. Finally our Sherman tanks load up with howling Maori troops, fighters who don't know how to stop. The Jerry line breaks open. One, Lieutenant Ngarimu, gets a Victoria Cross; they could've handed out a hatful.

So, on a trail of shattered strong points, we pushed the Afrika Korps into Tunis port and there they surrendered. The grey-blue Med at their back, their ships at the bottom of the harbour.

Bates pressed some of those wildflowers to send back to his troop. Slinger got cleaned out in a poker game with some Yanks. Harris mutters about the Almighty Dollar.

Monty drives past us, his black beret hung with regimental badges. This African campaign is over. There are rumours about invading France or Italy. The Russians have smashed the Germans at a great tank battle, called Kursk. Churchill says the tide has turned.

OUR DIVISION was being shipped home. Not me, still con-valescent — the doctors said I would make a full recovery. Slinger came and Harris, before they sailed.

Slinger said he would raise a glass to me at the first pub after they docked. Harris said I still had a lot to learn about the real fight, between capitalism and the workers. He left me his copy of *Das Kapital* (the communist bible) and from Harris, that's a medal. I did get a visit from our top guy, Freyberg. Said he knew my dad in the last lot.

Old Jacko. His ghost still haunts me.

Korea, 1951

THE END OF that war was a long way off then. The end of this one seems even longer. Hell — atomic bombs, hydrogen bombs, press-button warfare? We're the press buttons, I think.

Shanks is towelling his head and muttering about never being dry again. 'You going to the show tonight, Robbie?'

'What is it?'

'Some Yank musical, Singing in the Rain.'

'No, thanks.'

I want to do that letter to Teresa again. I've been trying to write it for months now. 'Shank, you can help me with something.'

He belches, rubbing his unshaven cheeks, and looks at me suspiciously. 'And what would that be?'

'We're going across to help those people pull their ox out. Couple of strong backs'll have it done in two twos'.

'You go. I'll cheer.'

'I've still got that can of peaches in syrup.'

'You blackmailing ratbag, Moran.'

I don't know why I want to help them. Maybe to stop thinking about the mess I left behind in New Zealand. Or maybe I'm still thinking about a girl in Italy who wanted to fly like a bird.

Italy

Italy, 1944

I NEVER KNEW it snowed in Italy, but it did; or that Italian winters were so bloody cold, but they were. Italy was sunshine and grapes, from where Mussolini sent his unwilling soldiers to fight. They ate a lot of spaghetti in Italy and the Pope lived there.

Slinger assured us that spaghetti grew on trees. Trees on a ninety-degree angle so the spaghetti could hang vertically for easy cutting. He said the Germans cut them all down retreating but, for a quid, he'd show us where one had been. No takers.

We're on the banks of the Sangro River, the division reinforced by a new intake. Fresh green conscripts, just like we were, who think they're tough because they did a hundred-mile route march in Egypt. They'll walk a damn sight further here — and up to their knees in mud. Fordham, who drove a Post Office van. Hopgood, who was in the Boys Brigade — oh hell, not another Bates. Stretton, a share-milker, and Haines, apprentice butcher. He'll see a different sort of blood and meat.

A lot of our old hands are fairly bitter about coming back. Furlough in New Zealand has opened their eyes. Well-paid, well-dressed Yanks are cutting a swathe through our women-folk. And lots of our young blokes are in 'essential civilian' jobs. Bates is especially bitter about all this; says girls under eighteen are seen in the streets with lipstick and makeup. What sort of an example is that to a troop of Girl Guides?

Apparently his blue-eyed Evelyn accepted a present of silk stockings from a Yank. But she'd put on a big dance for them so it was a 'thank you'. I say nothing.

So there was just about a mutiny when the Division was told it would be going back; organised and stubborn, needing other troops with fixed bayonets to end it.

Slinger was especially vocal. He'd picked up an MM in Tunisia on the Mesah Line. I asked why he came back and his reply was mostly swear words. Slinger had no intention of returning. Too many rackets and too many Americans with fat wallets.

'What're you on, Robbie, five bob a day?'

'More like four and sixpence.'

Slinger nods bitterly. 'Some blokes are getting that an hour at home. One bloody medal and they think I'm a good soldier.'

I said mistakes happen, but he would not be consoled.

Captain Shaw pulls me in for a talk. He wants me to go for officer training. Shaw's okay, one of those long-jawed, earnest blokes but he's not half as clever as Creel. I head-shake, there is no way they'll put those brass pips on my shoulders. Bates is offered the same deal. He accepts of course, it's his duty — and the scouts will love it, not to mention blue-eyed Evelyn. Maybe as much as those silk-stockings, I nearly say, but don't — he might be giving me orders one day.

So we settle down to a new 'theatre of war'. Theatre is a nice word but 'war' should be a four-letter word. The Italians are quiet, half-starved and scared. Mussolini hurt them, so did the Germans. Now we have come. Villages and towns are without water or power, everything destroyed by the Germans as they retreat.

Although 'retreat' is another nice word.

The Yanks made a landing at Anzio coast and were bogged down. And we advance, clobbering into strong point after strong point; they let us bleed, then pull back.

The rumour is they have something called the Gustav Line, which is anchored on a massive strong point. That they'll suck us in there and inflict losses that'll make Old Jacko's war look like an egg-and-spoon race.

We have a new company major — Milton, once a lawyer, sarky and up to our dodges. Should be, Slinger reckons, he's defended enough crooks in court.

I catch Milton one morning in a good mood. 'Sir, what're we doing in Italy?'

'We're fighting the German army, Moran. I'm sorry, has nobody seen fit to inform you? How remiss of us.'

He goes on to say they have coal-scuttle helmets and will shoot on sight, be careful. I let him. Rule one when getting information out of an officer — let him crack a cheap joke at your expense; puts him at ease.

'I do know about the Germans, sir. I mean us, the

En-Zedders. Why are we in Italy? Why aren't we fighting in the Pacific, you know, for home?'

Milton is shaving. He flicks lather from his razor before answering. 'Have to be fully re-equipped for that. Anyway, the Yanks and the Aussies have it all buttoned up.'

'Wouldn't our government rather have us home?'

He cuts himself and curses, dabs his face with a towel. 'They don't mind us here. Gives them a little more clout in Europe when the war is over.'

Milton is not in such a good mood now, but I push it. 'So why aren't we in France? We're trained in mobile warfare. Monty says he'll use us any time.'

'He did, Moran, in Africa and racked up the casualties. Anyway Freyberg says there's not the shipping.'

'They shipped the Div. back here, sir.'

'That was headed in the wrong direction, Moran. And so is this conversation.'

Soldiers don't concern themselves with politics. And politicians do not concern themselves with soldiers.

So … Italy.

Devil's eggs grenades

I FEEL OUT of place among all these new blokes; young and keen, but they've got a lot to learn about war. They're awkward around me, Moran, the tough desert hero. Geeze, what crap.

Some characters — Hopgood, call me Hoppy, who's got enough cheek to be Slinger's twin brother; Fordham, who thinks he's bullet proof and the next Charlie Upham. And while I'm licking them into shape, our new second lieutenant turns up. Straight out of the training course with actual creases on his trousers and shiny new pips, even shinier boots — until he gets out of the jeep, into the first puddle.

He comes over and I fire him my snappiest salute. 'Sarn't Moran, sir!' The new second lieutenant salutes back.

Slinger comes up, straight-faced, gives an even snappier salute, and I swear I hear his heels click. 'Sah!'

Second Lieutenant Bates salutes him back and makes to get his kit out of the jeep. But officers don't do that; I tell the driver to hump it to the tent. Bates motions me to follow.

'Yes, sah! Second Lieutenant Bates, sah!'

Bates stops at the tent, waits for the driver to go. 'Robbie, cut the crap, all right? I've got the rank, don't need to be reminded every damn minute. I was up for A Company but Fagan copped it.'

So I smile and put my hand out. He takes it, but the line is there. Non-commissioned and commissioned. He's an officer now and damned welcome to it. We chat a few minutes and talk about home. He went to see my mum, nice of him. She's got a scrapbook of the war and has kept all eight of my letters. He has a cake-tin from her.

Something's missing though, so I prompt him. Scouts … and Evelyn. Bates says the new troop-leader is a young teacher, excused conscription. And the boys are better at pestering Yanks for candy than learning reef knots and long splices. 'They'd have been more interested if I was a Yank with a pocket-full of bubble-gum,' he says.

Evelyn? Well, he proposed marriage (twenty-quid engagement ring!) but she wants to wait till the war is over. But she would wait for him. Bates has just about convinced himself she means it.

He's not the same Bates. Firm and even tough, gets his orders obeyed; even slaps Slinger down. Well, I never liked the angel Evelyn, and Bates's knockback'll make him a better soldier.

We've all changed and Italy is a different war. That we find out, soon enough.

Shortly after this, Slinger pulls me aside. He even offers me half a chocolate bar. He crunches his, brooding like the time in Cairo when his kings and queens were slammed by a running flush.

'What's on your mind, Slinger?'

'Bates. We've copped a real basket there, mate.'

'Bates is all right.'

Slinger gives me a look, like I'm the stupidest guy in Italy. 'He's come up through the ranks, Robbie. He knows all our dodges. We won't get away with a damned thing.'

'Of course you will, Slinger. Whenever did the Army out-think you?'

Slinger brightens at once. He loves a challenge.

Harris, of course, has a different view. The Div.

would not have come back if he had anything to say about it. I'm stripping the Bren and he drops down beside me. 'I don't like this, Robbie. The Brit establishment is infiltrating us.'

He's worried about long-term capitalist strategy. That's what he calls it. He says the Army is sucking in young blokes like Bates and turning them into officers. Making an officer-class that can be used in peacetime to crush the workers.

I can't buy into this but Harris is sure. In a few years time, when this war is over, the streets will be running with blood. Then we'll see blokes like Bates at the head of the new fascist legions. Harris is a good soldier, and tells me it's no use moaning to him when the capitalist heel is on my face. I promise not to.

As it happens, Bates is a good officer, although I fall over backwards trying not to call him 'sir' too often. He survives being a second lieutenant, too. Good in itself because the casualty rate among those boys is high.

Night. Dark outside and a cold wind flaps at the tent, promising a colder winter. Dark inside, just one torch on the map, our faces pale in shadow. I have a meal of greasy stew in my stomach and a whole string of things todo before I catch a few hours sleep. Same for Bates, unshaven with dark patches under his eyes that are not shadows.

He's lieutenant now, Shaw's down with dysentery. He traces his finger down the map and I notice the bitten nails. 'Here,' jabbing over one of the place-names. 'We have to clear the place out.'

There are nods and some resigned noises from the blokes. We've been expecting this. Slinger clears his throat and spits. Bates stabs the map again, remembers something. 'We can call in a cab-rank of Bostons. And we're to try not to damage the church. Some famous artist did the sculpture a few hundred years ago. If possible, don't bomb it to hell.'

'What if Jerry's in the church?' asks Slinger.

'We bomb it to hell,' replies Bates, and switches off the torch.

Panzerfaust

THERE ARE TWO real sods in this campaign, not counting the weather. One is house-clearing, fighting in those narrow-streeted Italian towns. The other is the SS.

There were no SS in Africa. The Afrika Korps were pro soldiers; we did our best to kill each other but there was respect. None with the SS. Elite fanatics, tough as those paratroops in Crete. They'll fight to the bitter end for their glorious Führer. Often, they take no prisoners. Sometimes, we don't.

So when an SS rearguard takes up residence in one of those little narrow-gutted towns — that's the biggest sod of all. When you have to go in and clean them out. That's when you're very good or very dead.

They've had a week to get ready and won't have wasted a minute.

We're company strength, two of the long-barrelled Shermans as back-up. They can match the Panzers but the SS here don't have one.

They do have the new Panzerfaust, a rocket-tube firing a damn big projectile. It makes a loud barking snort, like a bad-tempered dog. The first Sherman swings to one side, her treads unravelling like string. Her crew get out just before the second 'bark-snort' sets it on fire. The second goes up in flames, first time. The commander's cut down as he scrambles out; the others don't make it. They scream in the flames. My new boys are white-faced as they listen. Hopgood vomits suddenly, even more pale with shame. He needn't be.

This is what the hundred-mile march doesn't toughen you up for.

We work down the main street, door to door, keeping it very careful. I keep an eye on Fordham, he's bitten with the heroics bug that gets you killed — or your mates. There's a church ahead in the square so I keep an eye on that, too — there's usually a sniper in the belfry. Any townsfolk left will be huddled in their cellars.

The SS are platoon-strength; an M-42 set up ahead, waiting for us to get closer. Always very patient, these boys. We work doorway to doorway, covering the upper-storeys. The white-plastered walls are studded with bullet and bomb-marks; there's a defaced mural of Mussolini giving the fascist salute to a horde of goose-stepping Black Shirts.

At a house overlooking the square, we kick open the door and throw in a grenade. That'll set off any booby-traps waiting. Slinger and I are teamwork. I check upstairs and he does the cellar — better chance of finding wine there.

I go up the stairs. Incredible how silently you can tread in army boots when your life depends on it. Top landing, a bedroom door, kick it open. Someone there — shoot shoot. The figure shatters — my own reflection in a full-length mirror.

Slinger has come up behind. 'Steady, mate,' he mutters. 'That's seven years bad luck.'

That image — that wild look, teeth bared, the tense desperation — that was me. The mirror fragments crunch underfoot as I check the room. Lucky I'm not superstitious.

I check the square and the church. Nothing in sight, all quiet. Maybe the SS have pulled out. More like they want us to think that.

So on to the next doorway. Bates is leading a section from the other side. We signal silently. Be careful. Very careful. Too bloody quiet. Not even a dog.

So, right on cue, a dog begins barking, a high shrill yapping. A door opens, a black-shawled old lady comes fearfully out, followed by a younger one, also in black, both with scarf-wrapped heads, two kids and — a baby? No, the older woman's holding a yapping white puppy.

They scuttle down mid-street, ignoring our shouts, one kid in an oversize grubby white shirt, the little girl in a ragged pink dress. Their clothes flap, their feet patter on the cobblestones as they scurry, heads down.

We wait for them to get clear, pressed to the doorways. Across the street, Bates has just checked an alley and Hopgood skips across to the next house. He takes a peek in the window, presses up into the doorway. The door swings gently open behind him and he elbows it further open.

I open my mouth to yell — *Not like that! Grenade first!* — too late, he's stepping inside.

The explosion blows him out into the street.

This is what the SS are waiting for. All hell breaks loose — the scream of mortar bombs, that loud ripping-cloth sound of an M-42. At another doorway, I chuck a grenade in the window. From the way the door blasts into matchwood, there was another booby-trap there.

Bates, in the alley with two men, signals me to get upstairs. The two Italian women and kids are in a screeching terrified huddle by Hopgood's crumpled body.

No! Fordham is running out to help them. This is not the Boys' Brigade, you stupid sod! His flush of heroics is stopped by bullet-blast, ripping him open and flinging him untidily back onto the cobblestones.

'Slinger!' I yell and burst into the house.

He follows, unslinging the PIAT. He storms up the steps, nudges open the upstairs door. There's a bed by the window, a dirty mattress slashed open, the white flocking scattered everywhere. Some of it clings to the fine tripwire, which we were expected not to think about, having opened the door okay. We step over it, to the smashed window.

I peek around. Yes, there they are — the coal-scuttle helmets and a machine-gun barrel, next to Mussolini's toppled statue and the village fountain. I snap my fingers, Slinger has a peek, nods, fair shot. One eye on the tripwire, he readies the PIAT. They are buggers to load. You have to plant your feet on both sides and haul the butt back to fit in the big projectile. He has two. On one knee, he braces himself as he aims — they kick like a mule. He fires. A sudden deafening sound and the PIAT slams back to re-cock. Slinger's already fitting the next projectile. No need. The explosion has shattered both fountain and gun-crew. A bent gun-barrel sticks from the rubble.

Slinger gives the PIAT a loving pat. 'Worth quids on the black market, these,' he says.

We step back over the tripwire to the door. Downstairs, I throw a grenade back up and we take cover under the stairwell. After the explosion the bedroom ends up in the back garden — we were supposed to end there too. Bates, across the road, points up. He means he'll call in our cab-rank of Bostons.

Four two-engine Bostons roar down, one at a time, almost to rooftop level, the blunt noses bristling with machine-guns. They plaster the square with bombs and rockets, returning to strafe it. The church shudders, part of a wall collapses and the steeple falls with a loud crash. When the dust clears, we go forward, as carefully as before. The SS rearguard is still there — bits of them among the stonework.

The fountain has a shattered marble column, the base inlaid with brass wreaths and lettering. It's a World War One memorial to the fallen dead. Italy was our ally then.

Elly said that. I have to stop thinking about her and what happened.

Down the street, the women are dead. The kids are alive, eyes wide, their faces plastered with muck and dust. Their mouths are open but not making a sound. They just shake and shake as we bundle them away. The old woman appears to be moving. But it's only the little white dog crawling out from under her blood-soaked black skirts. It runs after the children, filling the air with high squealing whimpers.

In another town ahead, we'll be doing this again, soon.

British PIAT gun

SOMETIME LATER I go into the church. The bombs and rockets have left it a mess. A bright fresco around the walls, showing big-eyed saints in long robes, haloes like gold dinner-plates behind their heads, is now scarred and gouged by bomb fragments. Every stained-glass window is broken and the shattered fragments twinkle in the late afternoon sunlight as though all this ruin is scattered with different-coloured jewels.

They crackle and crunch as I walk up. The altar's overturned, a big crucifix lop-sided; a statue of the Virgin has half its face blown away, one arm broken at the shoulder. I pick up the hand — alabaster marble, beautifully sculptured, even to the fingernails.

Most of the long wooden seats are shattered. I sit in one that wobbles but stays intact. Soon the boys will be in, looking for kindling and communion wine but right now it's oddly quiet. A Catholic church and I am Catholic. 'Mickey Doolan' the other boys called me. It never meant a damned thing but somewhere to go on Sundays. Did sod-all to make Jacko a good parent.

But this is different. A different sense of things; sounds odd but that's what I feel. This was not just Sunday church to the townspeople. Wrecking it is brutal as — as the death of those women in the street. Boots scrunch on the fragments behind me.

Bates sits down, slinging his sten-gun in front as he does. 'Jerry's high-tailed it. Battalion coming up.'

'Smashing somewhere like this. It's not right.'

He drinks, hands me his canteen. 'You religious, Moran?'

'My mum is.' I'm still holding that alabaster hand. 'I just want to get through the war.'

'Then?'

I shrug. There is no 'then'. We get up, I glance at the altar and the broken Virgin. I don't think past the end of the war; just as I never thought about religion.

We leave the church. The first troop-carrier is coming down the street. Soldiers fill their canteens from the overflowing fountain. Bates gives me an amused look. 'Keeping that as a souvenir?'

I'm still holding the alabaster hand. I drop it and pull my tired mind around to the important things of survival. Like something to eat and a place to rest.

THIS TIME, we're headed down to the coast to sort out a supply problem. Shaw, our captain, is a good officer but a bible-basher to beat them all. If the lads get one more lecture about loose morals, I swear they'll go home.

There is cheap booze and women everywhere. Most of them are thin and half-starved with blank, hurt eyes. Doing this so their families can eat. Or because it's habit, a way of life.

The port has been bombed to hell, piles of rubble everywhere. The walls sometimes still standing, their windows also blank. Half-starved, ragged, jabbering kids everywhere. Smoke-stacks stick out of the oily littered water. There's the stink of raw sewage and that sweetish decaying stench of bodies, still unburied in the ruins.

'Will these people ever get their lives back?' breathes Bates.

'They brought it on themselves by following the Anti-Christ,' says Shaw.

It's that simple to him. But this 'anti-Christ', Mussolini, has been rescued by German paratroopers and heads some puppet regime up north. Up north, where rumour says the Germans are preparing defence lines that'll make Alamein and Mesah look like a row of sand-castles.

A black-haired boy appears in front of us, skinny, filthy, his face covered in sores, dressed in ragged shorts and a too-long army jersey, the sleeves cut short, a string around his waist. Shaw strides on, his jaw set. He's Methodist, so this Roman Catholic boy is practically a child of Satan anyway. The boy is not put off. 'Hey, money, smokes, food all good. Sisters all clean, like you men a lot.'

'Push off!' Shaw snaps. 'We're not interested in your sisters.'

The boy frowns but still skips ahead, a sort of infant Slinger, who never gives up. 'Okay, then, I get you my auntie, she good. Other women, all good, smokes, food, money —'

Shaw has had enough. He rounds on the boy, his chin jutting out, his eyes gleam with righteous dislike. 'Push off, kid! All we want here is the Harbour Master.'

The boy does duck back and we keep walking, Shaw stalking ahead of us. But the next moment, the boy ducks ahead, throwing his arms wide to stop us. 'Okay, I try and get Harbour Master. But more difficult! You better with Auntie!'

Bates the Scoutmaster has to hide a grin. Shaw goes bright red and keeps stalking onward.

It was Churchill's idea to attack through Italy. He called it the 'soft underbelly of the Axis beast'. Nice turn of phrase. Pity nobody thought about the mountains and rivers, the ravines. Bleak land made bleaker by the Germans. They blow up every damn thing they can, wreck everything they can.

They fight from strong points and move back. We think we've cracked their line, there's another behind it. Dug in, well defended until they move back — to the next line.

The villages we pass through are in ruins. No power, no good drinking water. The people huddle in their cellars without wood for fires. They are starving and even Slinger shares his rations without asking payment.

French, Indian, Polish, British, Americans, Canadians, ourselves. Must be like the barbarian hordes, says Bates. They are paying the price for supporting fascism, says Captain Shaw, our strict unforgiving Protestant. He doesn't care for me much — not that I care.

And all the time as we move forward, we hear rumours of a major German line ahead. The Gustav Line, and (they say) this is one we won't break. They've been working on it all summer and it's anchored on a mountain and a fortified monastery. Shaw snorts, can't see this place holding us up long. I hear its name for the first time.

Monte Cassino.

15 FEBRUARY 1944: A cold day and some cloud. We're down on the banks of the Rapido river. We have a good view of the big solid building on top of the hill. It's a monastery, looks more like a fortress. Monte Cassino.

The Germans hold all that high ground. Hangman's Hill, Cassino itself. Mount Calvario and Snakehead Ridge.

The north side of Monte Cassino plunges into a steep valley; beyond that, a tumbled mass of ridges, gullies and peaks; to the south, more mountains, stretching to the coast.

Monte Cassino is a German strongpoint. Interlocking defence positions, weapons pits and bunkers, artillery and Panzers. The river's dammed, turning the land to swamp. And among the defenders are our old mates of the Paratroop Corps.

An Indian division tried to take it, then the Poles and Brits. Now our blood will mix with theirs in the freezing mud. Word is, Cassino's packed with German troops and stores; their final redoubt.

'Bastards …' mutters Bates beside me.

He'd never have used that word a couple of years ago. But he's changed like we all do. And this whole campaign is one damn ass-kick after another. The Yanks went ashore at Anzio but their attack stalled at the beachhead.

The commanding general, Mark Clark, has a great opinion of his abilities — nobody else does. And he thinks we're 'fantastic fighting-men' — when he's not too busy making sure the news people get his best profile at the photo sessions. And his fantastic fighting-men look at that solid mountain fortress and know they're going to end up like the Poles, Brits, etc. before us.

Bates looks at his watch. He's white-faced, shaking a bit with some fever; we've all got bugs from the water. He hasn't talked about his bloody scout troop for weeks. 'Think we'll ever knock that bastard out?' he mutters.

A big maybe. From all accounts, the place is

massive. Built about a thousand years ago and every invader in Italy has gone past it — French, Saracen, Lombard, Spanish and Austrian — not that I bloody care. Or that it's a masterpiece of architecture.

It's in our way, it will cost lives; that's all I care about.

'Bates. Can you hear something?'

He's starting another letter but the paper is too wet and smeared with mud. He looks up, listens … shakes his head.

But I can hear something. A tingle I get, feeling sound before I hear it. Like the grey overcast sky is quivering. Air attack? But we have control of the air. Most of their airforce is fighting off the thousand-bomber raids flattening their cities, or on the Russian front.

It comes again. Another soundless quiver overhead like the sky has gasped. Something is happening — something is coming.

Now, Irwin, company runner, appears. Skipping from one point to another. One hand on his helmet, hunched over, repeating the same thing. 'Air raid, take cover, don't worry, they're ours.'

Ours ? Don't worry! Is the kid that green? Hell, we all duck for cover when the American bombers come overhead. They blast our side so often, rumour says Hitler's sent them all the Iron Cross.

Now comes the drone of the bombers, far away but audible. Slinger appears from nowhere, crams on his tin helmet. He lands beside us in the trench, scattering more mud over Bates, who curses. He never would have, two years ago.

We don't have long to wait. The engine-drone deafens, the first line appears out of the low grey clouds. Four-engine bombers, those 'Flying Fortresses'. They sweep overhead, followed by another line … another … then another.

'Cripes …' breathes Slinger, tilting his helmet, squinting upward. 'Cripes, oh cripes, there's no bloody end to them.'

Wave after wave is coming, I stop counting at a hundred and fifty. A deafening roar overhead and we flinch, but they keep going.

Suddenly their bombs are falling. Big bombs that howl shrill as descending hell.

The German anti-aircraft fire is rolling up. Thick red lines of tracer, exploding black puffs. One bomber staggers, smoke pouring from one engine. Now the thunder of exploding bombs mixes with the engine-noise. Each bomb is five hundred pounds of destruction.

Explosions bracket the monastery and the destruction starts.

Tons of high explosive are falling; massive sheets of red flame spurt upward. Now black and grey smoke rises in thick columns and blots out the red flame as more bombs fall. Line after line, the bombers drone overhead and the bombs still fall. Now the smoke billows thick and black, hiding all.

Not all land on their target. Some land near us and on the Indian division, earning exotic Hindu curses. Mark Clark's headquarters get bombed too, and that's worth a good laugh — later. Now the ground shakes and the explosions roll across the valley; the last bombs howl down and the smoke begins to clear.

The monastery is smashed to rubble but the high outer walls still stand. More aircraft, two-engine this time, fly in low. More explosions, the red flame lost in dark smoke, and those high walls tumble.

'Nice of them to give us warning,' mutters Slinger, shaking mud from his helmet.

The smoke is clearing on the hill, thinned away by the cold mountain winds. Now, where the big monastery stood, looking so solid, is just a pile of shattered stonework. A thousand years gone in a couple of hours.

Much later, we find out there were no Germans or stores in the monastery. Just the monks and civilian refugees; most of them are buried in the ruins.

I don't feel a damned thing. Neither do Bates or Slinger. They could bomb Buckingham Palace if it short-ened the war by a day.

WE HAVE TO paint over our silver fern symbol. A passing Brit sergeant cracks that we're painting out the white feather. Unfortunately he does so in hearing of Geary, who's built the way Mulligan was. After a knuckle-crunching moment, he's wishing he hadn't.

The Germans know we are coming. Aircraft drop propaganda leaflets on us. One shows Churchill and Roosevelt with a grinning soldier's skull behind them, saying Cassino is just the right job for the New Zealanders.

Another shows us in grass skirts and war-paint. A Maori gunner wanders over, outraged. Not only have they got their facts wrong but they're implying we're on a par with the Maori as fighters. He's built bigger than Geary even, so he doesn't get an argument.

We begin moving up. Past American troops in their green uniforms and funny bowl-shaped helmets. Past abandoned vehicles, some upturned and shattered; long strings of telephone cable on either side of the rutted muddy road.

Incredibly, there are still farmers in the fields — ploughing, digging, though the shells are whistling overhead. Refugees too, old tottering men, women with baskets on their heads and crying babies. A little boy with a too-large German forage cap on his head. Their faces are pinched and pale, fearful. They don't look at us.

Once a file of horsemen trot past. Bearded brown-faced men, big-nosed and fierce brown eyes. Helmets and striped robes, rifles in long leather buckets on their saddles. The Italian peasants scatter at the sight of them.

'Goumiers,' whispers our Brit guide. Irregular French cavalry from North Africa. They spare nobody — men, women or children; even the SS are scared of them.

Closer now comes the grumble of artillery; terraced rows of olive trees on the hills are broken and shattered. No farmers at work here; the muddy fields are shell-cratered, exposing hasty graves and decomposing bodies. The skies darken and it begins to rain,

Our first stop is Point 435. It's reached by a hairpin road covered by German artillery — like walking a tightrope under fire — three hundred yards from the outer walls of the town and castle, dominated by the wrecked monastery.

This is one place we will get to know well. Atop the hill is a wrecked pylon like a twisted steel gallows; Point 435 takes its nickname from this — Hangman's Hill.

Our Command has plans for the town. They made the monastery vanish. Now we'll see something we never want to see again. How to make a town vanish. It takes another thousand tons of high explosive — but they do it.

'God help the men under that,' mutters Slinger, who is not religious and doesn't like Jerry too much.

'It'll bloody settle them,' mutters Harris.

When the smoke clears, Cassino town is no more. It's shattered beyond recognition but the Germans are still there waiting. We still have to clean them out.

And whoever had the bright idea to bomb the town maybe didn't think that fighting among bomb craters might be difficult; or around heaps of toppling debris, twenty feet high; and steel girders, twisted and tangled like so much spaghetti.

Then the rain comes back. Rubble and dirt become thick and slimy mud as we work our way into town.

We're in another cold cellar, water's streaming down the walls and we're keeping quiet. There might be Germans next door; the building — all two walls and half first-floor of it — hasn't been cleared yet. Of all things, we get a mail delivery.

Another letter from Mum. She's heard it's very hot in Italy and have I eaten any grapes? Water drips from my helmet rim. I shiver, crunching a hard army biscuit. Grapes?

Bates reads his, sits a time, his eyes shut. Silently he passes it to me. The first time he's ever done that. Bates treasures his letters from Evelyn. But this one's from her dad.

> Dear Gerald,
>
> Evelyn has asked me to write this letter and I think the news is better coming from me. To come to the point, she's met a young man, fine young chap, a farmer. They're engaged to be married, will be by the time you receive this.
>
> Perhaps you should have pressed harder when you were back on leave. Faint heart never won fair lady! I am sure you will understand. Evelyn wants to settle down and surely she's entitled to that. With no end to the war in sight, I know you will understand. All the very best ...

So that was that; 'Dear John' letters, we call them. Bates takes it back, shreds and scatters it over the muddy floor. He has some more of her letters. They go on the fire, along with her photo.

The engagement ring? Evelyn decides to keep that.

We're pulling out. Not before time either. Our uniforms are muddy and ragged, we are crawling with lice. Rats are everywhere, glutted fat with dead flesh. The Germans have been pushed back to the castle, as filthy, lice-ridden and exhausted as us.

That night it's raining again. We're up to our ankles in freezing mud. The moon's hidden by heavy cloud and the only light comes from red and white flares, etching the broken stonework like a hell's landscape. They're laying white tape to guide our replacements in. As I turn to Slinger something drops, sparking and hissing, between us.

A German grenade.

Instinct takes over. You don't think, you react. Shoving Slinger I dive forward, grabbing the wooden handle. Swinging up the grenade, a sickening split-moment — *will it explode in my hand?* — then throwing it back into the darkness.

Explosion. The others react, unslinging their guns as the raiding party boils up from nowhere, stopped just long enough by their own grenade for us to be ready. A vicious scrambling fight erupts.

I go down, with two Germans on top of me. Slinger's rifle cracks one on his steel-helmeted head. I boot the other in the groin, his breath stinks on my nose as I wrest the machine-pistol out of his hands.

It's over, quick as it starts. Some dead, some wounded, one scrambles away. I pick myself up then sit down hard. Bates is beside me but I shake my head — just winded. And right on cue it begins to rain again.

Slinger curses. Bates is yelling to secure the prisoners.

I should be doing that, but I'm not. It's like a dozen things are happening inside me at once. This is black night, rain and mud, hand-to-hand fighting.

And suddenly I'm aware that this is how old Jacko fought — a meat-grinder battle like Passchendaele or the Somme. Trench warfare and fighting in broken hellscapes like this. Rats, lice and no sleep. Death waiting like that hissing grenade.

Slinger is asking if I'm okay. I nod but my helmet feels heavy as lead. He pulls me up, says I was a bit bloody slow with that Jerry grenade. Slinger's way of saying thanks. The order comes and we move out.

Still those odd disordered thoughts chase each other in my mind. Jacko's war and I'm Jacko's boy. It's like I'm in his skin, in this bloody freezing darkness. It took the death-stinking rubble of Monte Cassino to do it, but I understand him now — and the peacetime Jacko he became.

We grope on through the darkness, the white tapes trodden into mud. Jacko's boy. There are no tears in my eyes but I lift my face to the streaming rain and let it wash my face clean.

Panzerfaust

WE WERE ON the banks of another river now; Monte Cassino — what was left of it — long passed, the Germans retreating but never beaten. Intelligence says they are massing for a counter-stroke and they may have tanks.

Shaw dismisses this. 'Most you'll run into are a few stragglers. HQ says no way there are tanks.' There were.

Tiger Tanks are very bloody big and very bloody feared. They can swat anything we've got, at twice the distance; PIATS and the Yank 'bazooka' rockets just bounce off their 100mm armour.

Bates led us across an ice-cold river, thick with mist. Me, Slinger, Harris, and about six others. We steal forward through thick undergrowth and more of those endless stunted olive trees. The sun's rising and suddenly the mist thins away. We see the Tiger at the same time it sees us.

Fighting is one thing. Slaughter is another. Bates is too damned good an officer for suicide heroics. So the German soldiers come up and take our weapons. Our watches and cigarettes too. The tank just squats like an armour-plated elephant; one 88mm shell and they wouldn't even find the soles of our shoes. Now a German officer comes up, one of those silver 'gorget' things flashing around his neck.

We're stock-still, even scared, because rumour has it that one of those SS Divisions is in this area. *Das Reich* don't always take prisoners. This officer is tall, a scar down one cheek, from eye to jaw. That eye is filmed over and blind. The other is a sharp hostile grey. One hand is black-gloved, maybe has fingers missing. His long-barreled Luger's in its holster but the flap's undone. He pauses, looks at me, at my stripes and shoulder-flash. Nods grimly. 'Kiwi, ja ?' He points to his cheek-scar and eye. 'This in Crete.' Good English but guttural.

Paratroop. Pro soldier, not a crazy fanatic, so I take

a chance, he's of the Hitler Jugend. 'You must've landed near the Aussies then. We'd never let you get away that lightly.'

He looks at me. I hear an intake of breath from Harris behind me. The officer translates briefly to his men — then chuckles, a grim chuckle, but the tension eases. He nods, jerks his thumb backwards. Yes, and actually uses that expression we have heard watching those stupid war films: 'For you, the war is over.'

Bates just has time to rip off his officer pips so they'll keep us together. Which means the Jerries think I'm leading the patrol. I get compliments for my ribbons and a couple of kicks when I don't answer questions. Then a glass of schnapps. Frontline troops, we'd do the same for them. We even get a packet of fags.

I join the others outside. The Jerries push us into a barn and mount a machine-gun outside in case anyone gets an idea about running. We're told a truck will take us to a holding pen, then a train across the Alps to Germany.

We're all sullen, still coming to terms with it. Better than death, but that's about all. Slinger is the worst, sits in one corner, biting his lips. A little odd, because Slinger takes things as he finds them. Literally.

I go over and sit beside him, give him a fag, but he just nods, still muttering. Looks at me. 'You know that gold watch I got from the Eytie at Alamein? Silver hip-flask and cigar case from that Jerry after Alamein? Well, they took them, the lousy stinking thieves.'

I dare not smile. 'Slinger, you've got a packful of that stuff back at the camp. It'll be safe with our mates.'

Wrong thing to say. I get a bitter look. 'Safe? And do you think those light-fingered buggers will leave it alone? Rob a man blind, they would.'

I tell him that's the fortunes of war; explain that not everyone has his sense of values and if anyone can make a buck in the prison camps, then he will. Slinger just tells me to wipe that stupid grin off my face or he'll do it for me.

The truck comes and we're driven down an endless straight road, past vineyards, blue distant mountains against an overcast sky. Two guards have machine-pistols. At the other end, the guards have slant-lettered shoulder flashes — SS.

We stop at a railway station where a battered black locomotive waits, pulling a string of cattle-cars. The loco-motive belches white smoke, its boiler criss-crossed with welded patches where the US Airforce has used it for target practice. The cars have a mixture of Americans, British, Canadians, even a couple of guys in blue uniforms — Brazilians. We're loaded on board and the train shunts and jolts into jarring movement.

Bates has squeezed down beside me and waits till the wheels are clattering loudly on the track. 'We can have a couple of these floorboards up in no time flat,' he whispers in my ear. 'Drop through and be away. Hole up somewhere till our units catch up.'

I remind him that there's a flatbed car in front and

one behind filled with SS troops just hoping for some target practice.

'At night, of course,' he snaps. 'I'm not that stupid, Robbie.'

I nod. I don't know if I'll survive this war. Or if I'll marry and have kids. But I do know I'll never put one in a scout troop.

The train rattles like hell as it climbs the hill track. Smoke from the engine blows back, the damn dry hay swirls up as the night wind cuts in. All the blokes are coughing and sneezing, huddled in their blankets. Behind me, there's a ripping sound.

I think of something very rude and clever to say but Bates is still an officer. So I turn and he's pulled up the second length of plank. Icy darkness and the screech of wheels on iron track below.

'Are you seriously going to jump out? You'll get your legs cut off by the wheels and serve you right.'

'Then I'll get a disability pension. Come on, you wanker.'

'You're bloody mad.'

But, bundling up my blanket, I have to go. Bates fielded that grenade at Snakehead Ridge. I turn. 'Anyone else?'

No. They're too cold, too shaken, staring. Even Slinger, he just looks away. Bates is already jumping down. His boots scrape on the gravel, then he's gone.

And the train's moving, so I have to move fast, work

my way into the hole, splintered edges jagging my trousers. My boot-heels beat a tattoo on the sleepers. I tumble down. A bloody hard knock on my head, a frightful screeching blackness around me, then night sky and stars, and the train's going on ahead. I roll over. A guard on the roof in the moonlight, is looking up at the stars. He'll cop it when we're found to be missing. Sod him.

Bates is down the track, still on his knees, and I pull him up. He's okay, caught his head a bang on the sleepers. 'Let's get one thing straight, Bates. I'm not bloody "sir-ing" you while we're on the run like this.'

'You never did "sir" me. Come on, let's find a road.'

We somehow scramble down a steep gully. It's bitterly cold and we're both hungry as hell. Bates looks up at the stars. 'Bloody wonderful, aren't they? Milky Way — that's Orion's belt, all those the Milky Way. I learned all those in the scouts. Orion's Belt. The Great Bear, Milky Way.'

'Shut up about milk.'

We reach the road and start walking, heading back from the direction of the train, Bates figuring that last little town we passed through must be about a fifteen-mile walk. Oh, great.

We don't do the fifteen miles, of course — about half, then we're so tired and cold we have to stop. We huddle together under one of those little bridges that run over the ravines. Spiky little plants jab into us but we somehow manage to sleep a little.

And wake to a clatter of stones beside us. Two Italian soldiers in grubby overalls, with a jerrycan, are getting water at the stream. They've seen us at the same time. Both have rifles. One yells and a few more scramble down, look at us. One jerks his thumb up.

I give Bates a look and try not to sound sarcastic. 'That didn't last long, did it, Lieutenant Bates, sir?'

The Italians take us up onto the road. There's a small Fiat truck there, the radiator steaming. There are about six of them, privates and a non-com, unshaven and dirty, passing a bottle around; they look tough, though, and their rifles are clean.

They try a few questions and Bates answers in his limited Italian. He points at the track by the road, makes a train noise, mimes a jump. The soldiers laugh, even I grin. We get a swig from the bottle.

The non-com speaks. Bates frowns, mutters the guy has a South Italian accent you could cut with a knife. Something about Mussolini finally out of the way. Their battalion forced to work for the Germans so they've decamped. On their way to join the partisans.

And they can't be bothered with us. Radiator filled, they all get back into the truck. Toss us a bottle of wine, half a long sausage and a loaf of bread, yell some longwinded farewells, and the truck heads off. We wave back and, next moment, our mouths are full of sausage. Garlic and horsemeat probably, but an old boot would taste good right now. We empty the wine-bottle and refill it at the stream. It's another hot morning and the flies are buzzing. Bates is thinking hard.

'Our train was headed for Germany. Mussolini was running some kind of puppet-state up north, must have been knocked over.' He suddenly grins. 'Anyway we're still free, eh, Robbie?'

About four miles on there's a brutal reminder that the war is still going. There's the Fiat truck, overturned and riddled with bullets, those Italian soldiers dead around it. From the empty cartridge cases, they put up quite a fight.

I reach down and pick up a matchbox — empty, boot marks all around it. Red-covered with a black eagle and German lettering. Obviously the owner of that match-box and his mates weren't too happy seeing Italian soldiers taking it on the lam.

Italy might be out of the war. Germany was not.

Devil's eggs grenades

WE HEAD FOR the hills. In the distance, once, we hear the sound of artillery or bombs. And there are plenty of Germans around. Once a convoy of half-tracks waddle past, crammed with men.

In the foothills, we come to a village. Just a small one, off the road. As we approach it a distant rifle cracks and a bullet whangs off the rocks ahead. The message is plain. Sod off. The people here are scared. Already some of the partisan bands are fighting each other. We follow the road higher. Bates is limping badly. He jokes that there was nothing in the scouts guidebook about this — until lately he hasn't mentioned them in months.

In another small village ahead some hens are clucking. That's a good sound; we haven't eaten for two days. And if anyone takes a pot at me, I'll break the damned rifle over his head.

Nobody does. I learn later that the village below was visited by partisans who liberated their food stocks. This one was by-passed. Or maybe they can see we're just a pair of ragged-ass Allied soldiers. But as we approach, someone shouts at the barking dogs and an old priest hobbles out and raises his hand.

Monte Bianco is a poor hill village with drystone walls, a few thin goats and sheep, some stunted olive-trees and sparce crops in the stony soil; a straggle of little white-plastered houses and a smaller church.

The cottage we're in is one-roomed, a couple of lofts overhead for sleeping. There's a shrine to the Virgin Mary, a rickety table and chairs. Bates is white-faced and gasping with pain when they get us into the room. We are given a meal of bread, goat-cheese and olives and find out later they go hungry that evening.

There are almost no young men in the village. In this house, there's a sharp-faced old grandma, two girls wrapped in black shawls, an old white-whiskered man — uncle to the girls I think — and the priest. He and Bates manage a conversation.

Bates sits up, wincing as he does. 'Robbie, know what this old bloke wants? Wants us to stay and help.'

'What?'

The Germans have been raiding these villages further along the mountains, taking what they want and levelling them so the partisans have nowhere to go. There are no partisan bands near here but they're destroying them, anyway. Villagers who don't escape are killed.

The priest repeats, 'Morto, *morto*,' and sketches an outline on the table with a lump of charcoal. A skull and crossbones —the Death's Head, our old mates of the SS.

'What are we supposed to fight them with?' I look at the priest and make a shooting gesture, clicking my thumb on an imaginary trigger. 'Rifles … guns …?'

The priest nods — Father Tommaso is his name — says something quickly to the white-whiskered old boy who leaves. Father Tommaso speaks again, Bates interprets. The partisans took just about anything that resembled a weapon.

The old boy returns with an armload of stuff he dumps on the table. A rifle and pistol and — Bates and I jump, to stop the other three items rolling off the table — 'Red Devils'. We stop them very gently.

I can see why the partisans left these behind. The guns look useless, the Red Devils too dangerous. Bates picks up the pistol — a revolver — pitted and old, the barrel-grips missing, the cylinder jammed with rust. He taps the barrel and rust gathers in a neat brown pile on the table. Father Tommaso speaks again. Bates nods.

'He says they're quite old.'

Yes, they are quite old. I pick up the rifle, manufacture

date stamped on the breech: 1898. A Carcano breechloader, a handful of bullets that looks too small. Not so much rust comes out of it, but it looks just about as useless as the pistol.

And the Red Devils — three dented cylinders, the red paint chipped — a type of Italian grenade that works on some kind of long firing-pin. You can blow yourself up just by holding them the wrong way.

The old boy and the women watch in silence as we look at the weapons. The older girl — a young woman — looks at me with big brown eyes until her mother nudges her.

I try the breech-action and the rust-pitted knob scratches my palm. The bullets do fit, the bolt scrapes clumsily back. Fifty years old and will hit anything it's not aimed at.

'Do we have a choice?' mutters Bates.

We don't. He's too hurt to go on and — unless I miss my guess — is nearly down with fever. And there's something about these people. They're scared but too proud to beg.

So we nod, okay. The priest mutters something that sounds like a blessing. The oldest daughter gives me a fleeting smile, gets another nudge.

Bates tries the rifle, too. 'You'd be better off with Momma's kitchen knife,' he says,

And we find somewhere very safe for the grenades.

Devil's eggs grenades

BATES DOES come down with fever and spends a week shaking it off. One of the old women sits beside him, dabbing his forehead with a rag soaked in cold water. They're not short of cold water in Monte Bianco — but short on everything else.

The two older women are Maria and her sister Aniella. Their husbands, and all the able-bodied men of the village, were rounded up for military service or forced labour. The grandfather is Teodosio. The girls are Mirella the older, Teresa the younger.

Mother Maria and Sister Aniella are a type I know. Like those Cretan mums; the same sharp black-eyed faces. They are glad to have us but if we touch their daughters, we're crow-bait.

They have little enough to eat, too. A few scraps of vegetable cooked in oil, hard bread, olives, some cheese — now and then an egg. I spend my time stripping and cleaning the Carcano; at least till I can work the bolt without it grinding like rocks.

Because I'm Catholic I rate a couple of points higher than Bates. They've never heard of scouts either. Mirella sometimes manages to do her chores near me but Mother or Auntie is always hovering around. Father Tommaso talks a little, but luckily my Italian doesn't allow deep questions. I think he senses my lack of faith. He pats my hand and smiles.

No sign of the Germans. But we know they will come.

Father Tommaso has found a jam tin of the old bullets; about half look usable. Every afternoon I go up the mountainside and squeeze off some shots, setting the sights, getting to know all its cranky ways.

The cold wind cuts at my face, but will take the noise of my shots away from any Jerry patrol in the lowlands. I set up rocks, pace off and begin firing. The Carcano makes a flat 'clap' sound, caught in flatter echoes.

A bloody awful gun. The butt kicks like hell against my shoulder, the bolt sticks. It fires way to the right. Solid though, and even well made. In the right hands, it will kill.

My hands. They will have to be the right hands.

I'm at the bottom of a slope and sprawl down for one last shot. The loose stones slide around me; one hits my shoulder. I sight along the barrel and think of my father. His Mannlicher was made by the same people who made this — but better. Another stone hits me and I curse. Every damn rock on this mountain is moving.

I squeeze the trigger. Clap. The distant rock topples over. So the sights are as good as I can make them. For when I have to line up a *Das Reich* stormtrooper.

Another stone bounces off my head — damn! I turn around. Mirella is sitting on the ridge above me, another pebble poised in her hand, a wicked smile on her face. She's in a long brown dress with a black shawl around her shoulders; long hair swinging loose under her scarf.

I go back up to the ridge, my feet sinking in the scree. I sit down beside her and she keeps smiling. But we're both wary. She's broken every rule of womanhood coming to see me alone. But mindful of her mother's long kitchen knife, I am a perfect gentleman.

'War finito … you go home …?'

It was a little surprise to know Mirella spoke some English. Her uncle taught her before the Germans took him. Seems she has a cousin in the Queensland cane-fields, whom she was to marry. But he married a local girl and Mother Maria spits at the mention of his name.

'Home?' she repeats.

New Zealand? I'm on a brown and grey mountain-side in north Italy, and even south Italy seems distant. And Aro Street, Wellington, the little weatherboard house? Like it never existed.

Maybe Dad thought that in the trenches. I never knew him, never liked him and still don't. But somehow, after Monte Cassino, he's closer. I blink and the cold air hits me. Mirella is watching as though something showed in my face. Her cool fingers touch my hand.

'Think of home, people there?'

People? She means do I have a girl. I shake my head, feeling like a big clumsy lout of fourteen. Like the first and only time I took a girl to the pictures. Maureen Sullivan, and I spilt the Jaffas all down the theatre floor. 'Ah … not pretty girl like you.'

She adjusts her shawl and looks away. The little smile's still there; maybe that pinkness in her cheeks is from the cold mountain wind. Some of the blokes would be trying it on now — and getting their eyes clawed out, because it's so far and no further with these north Italian girls. I smile.

'Girls here are very pretty. You are pretty.'

That was more clunky than working the breech on my Carcano. Her cheeks blush a deeper pink and there's a sparkle in those dark eyes. The ends of her shawl flutter like wings as she stands on top of the ridge. She spreads her arms wide and cries out.

'Look! I am flying!'

The high peal of her voice rebounds from the slopes. Her face is flushed, as though in this perfect moment — with all the mountainside below — she is fully alive, completely free from fear.

'Mirella!'

I know that voice with the harsh screech of a crow and go to ground, as if from the tac-tac-tac of a machine-pistol. It's Mirella's mum, looking for her daughter.

Mirella flutters again, this time like she's back in the pigeon-loft. Not a glance at me as she turns and waves, picking up her basket with a casual swing. She's been collecting wildflowers. Not a glance back as she scrambles down the mountainside.

It's late afternoon. I should be getting down too. But if I follow Mirella, it'll be a dead giveaway. I'll be dodging mother's knife and grandpa's stick. So I stay put for an hour.

A long bloody cold hour. I work the pull-through on the barrel. At least no more rust is coming out. At least now, it will kill. And it will have to if *Das Reich* come this way to mount their last defence, the Gothic Line.

First, they have to wipe out the partisans to secure their supply routes. And the quickest way to do that is wipe out the little villages that might support them, as they did on the Gustav Line.

They will come.

I think about this an hour, huddled against the ridge, while the wind blows colder. I think about Mirella till my teeth chatter. Then I make my way down the slope. It's dark when I get to the village, frozen to the bone.

Mirella is sewing in the corner with her mother. Grandpa gives his whiskery smile and Auntie puts down a bowl of vegetable soup and a slice of black bread. I wolf it down, using Bates to tell them that the rifle works fine. Grandpa chuckles and nods, already imagining the heaps of SS dead. More like a few shots to keep their heads down while the villagers escape.

Bates is nearly over his fever, goes to sleep. They want me to go down to Monte Bello in the morning and persuade them to up stakes and come up here — where the fearless Kiwi will defend them.

Suddenly I notice there's a lot of smiling going on. Mirella does not smile, but her tight lips want to. Teresa does but a sharp look from her mother wipes it off. And Maria, and even Aniella, show a glimpse of white teeth between their thin lips. Like they know something.

Then I get it.

She knows why Mirella went up the mountainside. She knew I was up there — also that I froze an extra hour before coming down, no doubt she had a quiet snicker about it while she sat by the fire.

So, straight-faced, I thank her for dinner, get a smooth '*grazie*' and roll up in my blanket beside an already snoring Bates. It's a long walk down the mountain tomorrow.

Mirella. I do like her. There's something different, young and innocent about her. And I know she likes me. Even after Elly, I don't know much about love. But it feels good to think about Mirella. And thinking about her, I fall asleep.

It was an easy walk down the mountain. I chewed on salty olives and thought, why even go home? Mirella liked me and I think her old mum did. It might be different when the young men returned. Old Father Tommaso just shrugged and said, wait.

And sooner or later the war would bloody find me — officers telling me what to do and where to go. I stop, looking around at the stubbly green plants among the grey slaty rock, the cold pale blue sky overhead. I feel free up in these mountains. Maybe the war won't catch up.

And thinking that, I hear that first distant little rattle. And the cold wind that brought the noise up chills me back into the real world. Monte Bello was still half a mile away over the rise. I run up, my footsteps making the stones loudly slide and rattle.

Ahead a sudden trace of smoke rises into the blue.

Not yet — not now!

But, yes, here and now. Below, the war has caught up with Monte Bello, a little scrape of stone houses like Monte Bianco. There, crawling among the houses, are three half-tracks, spotted with green and brown camouflage, like big, steel-plated slugs. Smoke is coming from all those white-plastered cottages and rising more thickly. And along one stone wall are the huddled bodies of old men, women and children.

'SS' is slant-lettered on those carriers. So they are here, the troopers in shirt-sleeves and weapons shouldered. Strolling around, eating and shouting to each other. One man goes down a line of tethered goats and mules, shooting each one. Now the barns are set on fire. Dead animals are dropped into the well. No food or shelter, no water; *Das Reich* do their job like the trained professionals they are.

Now, watching, I hear shouted orders clearly on the thin air. Soldiers pile into one carrier; it lurches into growling life on the upward trail.

There's only one little village ahead, one vehicle is enough for the work of destruction. A few more men, women and children — and goats — to kill. The stones scramble loudly underfoot as I turn and run.

I can still remember that run. The worst long minutes of my life still come back in nightmare. Running up the track, past the stunted olive trees that those caterpillar tracks will crush. Oh geeze, oh for Slinger and his PIAT — we'd make scrap iron of that carrier —

I'm running uphill, my chest in a tight band, gasping in the thin air that dances black spots before my eyes; sweating, the leather strap rubbing, my useless obsolete gun jigging on my back. Behind me, the distant growling is getting louder as the weapons-carrier grinds slowly up — and up. In low gear, taking its time, no hurry.

The track curves towards the village ahead, that growling grows louder behind. A woman is milking a goat, two children are making a ball of wrapped paper. Old men sit on the benches outside their homes. Late Sunday afternoon cooking smells hang in the air.

I'm running, bone-tired and sweating, bawling from a hoarse dry throat. 'They're coming!'

A sudden silence, even the goats stop bleating. No need to say who 'they' are. And in that silence comes the horrible engine-growl. So they're out, the old men waving their sticks, the women fluttering their black shawls, like hens scattering.

Father Tommaso's voice, shouting to run — *run!*

A bundle of possessions snatched up; children screaming; a man with a bleating kid on his shoulders; a woman with two squawking hens in her arms. Mirella runs towards me but her mother catches her hand.

'Roberto, Roberto!'

I'm unslinging my rifle, flapping a hand at her — get back! Looking around, shouting. 'No animals' noise!'

Father Tommaso catches on, shouting. The hens and goat are cast down, now Bates is out, supported by Teresa and her mum. He's got that bloody antique revolver. 'Moran, I'll stay with you!'

Like hell! 'Get moving —I can't look after you and fight the Huns.'

Huns. What my old man called them. He's yelling — *forget being a hero, Bates, and sod all scouts* — he'll get us both killed. I'm no bloody hero, not letting that happen. The growling is louder.

One chance, a good one. The villagers can scatter among gullies and caves, it'll take *Das Reich* forever to winkle them out. So me and the Carcano will draw them on, over the other side of the mountain.

One chance.

They'll be relaxed, their last stop, no trouble expected. Even a few unlikely ragged-arse partisans won't bother them.

Maybe one ragged-arse Kiwi soldier will.

I leap over a stone wall ahead, like the one those Monte Bello villagers died against, and up the wide scree slope. No cover but that's good, the Germans have to see me.

Now — suddenly and too soon — that armour-plated slug lumbers into view. The German troopers see what they expect — villagers scattering, animals and birds bleating and squawking. The gunner, swinging his M-42, sends a sleeting blast after them.

Bates goes down, rolling over and over — *geeze, were you looking for a merit badge? Useless, waste* — and suddenly I'm thick with cold fear.

No — not this!

Mirella has broken from her mother and is running back. I will never know why. Maybe that fear in her dark eyes when she talked about her cousin — maybe to distract them from me. She didn't; they were too well-trained for that. Just one trooper turns, raises his Schmeisser. Tuc-tuc-tuc. The flat sound echoes clearly over the mountain.

Mirella stiffens to the bullet. The impact makes her arms fling wide. Like the time she stood on the ridge and said she was flying. Now she crumples and falls, slipping down among the sliding scree; sliding among the stones, arms and legs all ways, into a tangled heap. An untidy limp tangle of arms and legs.

I am watching from the higher slope. Watching Mirella die. German bullets around me — because they have not stopped. Even so, my body is somehow rigid, it takes an effort to throw myself down.

She is dead — dead — *dead for me!*

More bullets splatter their lead on the rocks, the troopers closer. All feeling gone among this dead bare rock. The officer, that silver ornament-thing flashing at his neck, shouting, pointing to me. Get him, *raus — raus!*

Raus, raus!

I was eleven when Aunt Francesca bought my little brother the monkey. A mechanical toy, banana in hand, in red tunic and round red cap. Clockwork was really something then. Wound up, it bounced over the floor, jigging the banana. The sound of that idling carrier-engine's like the chatter of the monkey.

We all had a try, my sister, me and Michael, my mother smiling as she wound it up again — *watch how it bounces over the floor, dear!*

Watch how it bounces over the floor!

Why should the image come so sharply to mind? Click-click-click, but it's as if the noise is lost in thick deep jelly. Then awful hot-cold fire, the rising anger, takes over, flooding me with uncaring murder.

Who do you think you are dealing with, some peasant with a gun? Well, you think that, because I am no ragged-arse bumbler. I bring up the Carcano, a snapshot. That Schmeisser-guy spins around. His helmet rolls down the slope, his body behind it.

Get the message, eh? *I'm a soldier like you!*

Pulling those awful grenades from my pocket, just as likely to blow me up, I hope like hell they are working. The first two, one in each hand. I hook out the pins, throw one, then the second. *Three — four seconds on the fuse?* The first grenade explodes, then the second —

Hell ! Another bloody great explosion — better than I dared hope for. Grenade fragments must have punctured the petrol-cans on either side of the carrier. The gunner leaps out, through thick red-orange flames and bulking black smoke, rolling over the ground.

And I flick out the long brass pin of the third grenade, throwing overarm, hearing my old cricket-teacher yell — *put some ginger into it, Moran!* Now they're getting up and turning. Well, it worked — now they're after me!

Another explosion, they go to ground. But when they get up, five still lie there, two tossing around in agony, others still, the driver burning. I snap-shoot and another pitches over.

There are still six of them left. Logic says I should retreat, using cover, draw them up the slope. Logic says I am out-numbered and must die. But logic does not possess me like that awful clockwork flame or scream a cold searing hate. Those things push logic aside and take me down the slope, firing as I go.

Now the bullets are snickering around me. I note

their buzzing — detached — like they're flies. The old Carcano kicks my shoulder again, I slip on some rocks. A good thing, because just then the bullets whack where I was standing. *Raus!* That officer shouting, the silver chest-thing — gorget — flashing, directing fire.

On the ground, rolling towards rocks, elbows scraping raw as I steady and fire. That gorget blinks, flicks away, the officer is flung backward. I slip in a new bullet, wincing as that rust-pitted bolt jabs my raw palm. Click — *a dud!* Wince again as *I work the bolt, eject the bullet and blink angry cold tears.*

Another whiplash of bullets, more shouting. But something is wrong, those shouts are uncertain. There are just four left now and one is running away. Another, a sergeant I think, *Feldwebel*, shouts, but he keeps running, so the *Feldwebel* shoots and the trooper stumbles, goes down.

As the *Feldwebel* turns back, my bullet neatly puckers the SS insignia on his helmet. Now there are two, one of them on his knees, wounded.

You killed Mirella! Still feel like the master-race, muckers?

My clothes are torn from the rocks, my face, hands and elbows running blood, I'm forking that clumsy bolt shut and standing. In range of their machine-pistols now, but the standing trooper must adjust, bring his *Schmeisser* around — and die as he does.

Which leaves one, on his knees, one arm wet with blood, trying to reload his machine-pistol one-handed, fumbling with the clip, his face white, his mouth open.

I can just about hear his breath hissing, I can see his eyes glaring under the helmet-brim.

If this was North Africa, he would put down his gun. I would give him a drink from my canteen and put a field-dressing on his shattered arm. But this is not North Africa. I am on a cold wind-swept mountain in Italy and Mirella is dead. And that awful brutal rage is still pounding its cold shockwaves.

I stop.

He's fumbling that new clip. Thickset, fair-haired, his blue eyes like ice. Ramming the clip in like the trained soldier he is — knowing I will never let him use it. *Mirella — she never had a chance.*

So I wait. I want him close to life before I kill him. He cocks the pistol as I bring up my Carcano.

Crack!

And all at once, there's nothing but a rising sick horror in me as he falls forward. I want to vomit as he drops his machine pistol and his helmet clatters, rolling down the slope. I clench my bleeding hands tight.

It's over.

The wind shifts, blowing smoke from the burning carrier in my face. My eyes sting and water. Somewhere there's the smell of burning flesh from that gunner. And it's over — over. I am drenched cold as if walking through a waterfall and the whole damned mountain tuens its cold stone face on me.

Disordered little thoughts like getting out of a bad dream … Hearing the moans of those wounded men … My shoulder aching from the recoil of the gun. *A rifle Moran, not a gun!* Yeah, but you got your head blown off, Sergeant Seaton, remember? I'm not peeling any more spuds.

Walking further down, skidding, because the rock-scree catches like a tripwire, I stop by one of the wounded. A bullet under his shoulder, no blood on his lips so it missed the lung. But he needs the expert care he will not get. He mutters something in German. A plea for help? More likely 'shoot me!' because he knows he is finished.

I don't know him. I have no intention of shooting him. Nor of saving him. The villagers are back, they have seen Mirella die, the women keening with distress and anger.

His pain-filled blue eyes follow that sound. To where the black-clad women are coming, their long frocks flapping in the wind, black scarves wrapped around their white faces, old men in their baggy trousers and black jackets, white-bearded.

The pain-filled blue eyes come back to mine. They are coming to kill you, say my eyes back. Because you came to kill them and you did kill Mirella. And I cannot save you because I am sick of killing. So I walk — sleep-walk — on down. Another trooper is stirring and moaning, fingers scrabbling in the gravel. Over to the left, one is tossing sideways in his own blood.

I'm a sleepwalker; their pain has no meaning.

Now, I'm passing through the line of black-clad women and white-whiskered old men, Aunt Aniella at their head. Her long sharp face is set like ice, like a cold snow covered mountain, the knife in her hand. She does not glance at me.

I walk over to Mirella, kneel and straighten her arms and legs. Her eyes are shut, long-lashed eyelids on cheeks, her red-lipped mouth open a little. She looks peaceful; the glint of a silver crucifix in her torn blouse.

Father Tommaso is up, pushing me urgently aside. He has business, the last rites. He kneels. I stand, still cannot cry, although the smoke-sting is in my eyes. Mirella is dead. Bates is dead. All my hurt is spinning in slow thick, waves, becoming faster. A shrilling distant sound in my ears tells me the wounded SS are dying under those pitiless knives.

I think Father Tommaso is talking to me. But that's lost in the spinning pounding blackness —

Bren gun

I HAVE NEVER seen the sky so strangely shaped; or that olive-green colour, set with dark flickering shadows — and how crazily the sun swings in that slanting sky. I'm shaking, ice-cold trickles, then suddenly hot. Shivering and moving; from somewhere comes a retching gasping noise.

I can't load my bloody gun, the clips fall and crash like tinny thunder. Harris, you bugger, stop gaping. Can't you see the SS are coming up the hill? Hell, that bloody

stupid gun of mine is falling apart and Mirella is screaming my name. Somebody is screaming.

No, those nine hundred Alamein guns explode with
eye-popping thunder. We are there in the black storming
fire, the tank is on fire — *shit, Lieutenant Creel, don't stare
at me, that 88mm* —

More darkness and red blobs that wring me out, I'm
smacked hard around, that Hurricane bursting into the
ground — keep up, keep up! The desert's hot and I'm sweating cold and that old Carcano's thumping my shoulder —
hell it hurts when I pull the bolt-lever back.

'Hey, Robbie, you back with, us?'

A voice I know. That swaying sunlight is a light bulb;
the olive sky is a tent roof. And I've never been so weak or
sweat-soaked, my eyes gummy and voice cracked in a
sandpaper throat. My chin stubble rasps on thick woollen
blankets. There's a bed under me and I turn, clutching the
blankets. Someone is sitting beside me, he grins — Slinger!

'Stop pretending, you lazy skiver.'

Slinger. The same grin, fag in the corner of his
mouth, he's pouring something out and I drink it. Nearly
choke, it's fizzy and sweet — Coco-Cola?

Slinger grins. I'm in a field hospital outside Rome.
He says a Yank patrol pulled me out of some village, full of
fever. The same Yank battalion stopped their train, so he,
Harris, Gumboot, and some others went looking for me.

'We heard about this mad Kiwi who took on the
whole SS. Reckoned it had to be you,'

'So you know Bates is dead.'

Slinger's drinking from the Coke bottle. Chokes,

looks at me. He shakes his head, closest I've seen to a good smile on his face. 'Bates? No, they got him in the leg. In a hospital ship, lucky beggar, going home.'

Bates is alive! He came through. That deep pounding blackness comes on me, lit with memory-fire. I open my eyes again.

Harris, this time. Seems I slept the night through, still limp as wet rags. Harris had heard about the village fight. Says it's time I took the workingman's side. He's even brought chocolate, the nutty Yank stuff I like. Feeds it to me a piece at a time.

'You're not too bad, Robert. Just too damned mixed up.'

Harris is talking about politics. I'm thinking personal because I am thinking about that village, Mirella flying. Harris is tucking the blanket under my chin.

'Get to sleep, old lad. You're on your way home.'

British Piat gun

Homecoming, 1945–46:

HOME SOMEHOW frightens me. Perhaps because it is so normal. The stairs still need that paint-job I promised to do in 1940. The third step still creaks and wobbles; the old coir mat and Mum's battered gumboots.

My kitbag hits the verandah with a thud — *then* I remember the Madonna statue I bought for Mum. Hope it's not broken, think of a wrecked church and alabaster hand. I raise my own hand and knock.

Hell, I was in a dozen battles. Alamein and Cassino, took on whatever Jerry could throw at me. And yet I pause, can't resolve to knock. Then remember I live there, so I just turn the rattly brass knob and walk in.

The door-frame nicked from my pocket-knife; the threadbare hall carpet; that print of the Lourdes Grotto, still lopsided. These things scare me more than the growl of oncoming Panzers … because they are there, like — like nothing happened.

Down the corridor is the kitchen. Mum will be there.

She wasn't at the dockside. Well, maybe she didn't get the telegram. Just crowds of people, shouting and embracing. I pushed my way through them, feeling alone as hell.

She's sitting with her back turned, her dark hair almost grey, coiled on her neck, in that shapeless old blue cardigan. She's shelling peas.

'Hello, Mum.'

She turns, almost unsurprised. She puts the bowl on the table and we hug. It's formal and clumsy, nearly hurried, we each take a step back.

'You look very thin, Robert. I expect you'd like a cup of tea.'

I put my kitbag against the dresser. The old chipped cups and plates tinkle as I do. Father used to smash them in his rages.

Now she's filling the kettle, lighting the gas, talking like I was someone dropped in for a chat. 'I must have got the ship wrong. How did you get on, overseas?'

How did I get on? Well listen, Mum, I saw this boot once, with a decomposing foot in it. I saw a tank crew burned to cinders. Young Ernshaw got disembowelled, my company CO was cut in half — *are you listening!* No, you are not, because the words are locked on my tongue.

'I've got some gingernuts, Robert. You like those.'

Mum, I've forgotten about gingernuts. Army hardtack, spread with jam and flies, fancy crunching that down? And army tea, goes a muddy yellow when you add condensed milk. And Tilly was just suddenly dead, Sergeant Seaton's head blown away — *the blood was so bright!*

Mirella. Will I ever be able to mention her name aloud? *She wanted to fly —*

'Are you still milk and two sugars?'

227

They killed Mirella so I went down the hillside and killed them all. No, some wounded, left those for the knives. I can still hear their screaming — *Ernshaw screamed, drumming his heels* —

'Robert, sit down and be comfortable.'

I want to be on my knees, hugging her tight. I want to weep hot tears and scream and scream how bloody awful it was, shit — *shit* — I want to howl like a gut-shot dog. But the wooden case that is my body sits stiffly down. My wooden head nods, my wooden lips say something.

Suddenly the tea is spilling from an overturned cup. I only moved my hand but the enamel bowl is rolling over the floor and peas are spilling everywhere.

Did I sweep it off? In that single violent movement, become my father's son? Driven by an awful explosion of horror and panic, wrenching me apart like a bursting shell? And she flinches, because that was Jacko's anger.

'I'm sorry, Mum. Haven't been well.'

'I know, son. Never mind.'

Maybe Jacko apologised a few times before fuelling his anger with alcohol. She's a casualty too, I have to remember that. So when she goes to the floor to pick up the peas, I kneel too. I even pat her shoulder and hope the hell her Madonna is still in one piece. She'll like that.

'Your brother and sister are at the Church Camp. I've got a nice casserole for dinner.'

'No peas, Mum! Not after they've been on the floor.'

It wasn't much of a joke, but I think she understood why I made it. Anyway, she smiled.

His Majesty,
King George the Sixth
is pleased to announce
the award of the
Victoria Cross to
Sergeant Robert Francis Moran, 9033,
New Zealand Division.

During operations in Greece, Crete, North Africa and Italy, this soldier showed constant heroism under fire and indifference to danger. He received the Military Medal and the Distinguished Conduct Medal for his exploits in Crete and Mingar Qaim, North Africa.

Subsequent to this, at El Alamein, Sergeant Moran engaged and eliminated an anti-tank gun emplacement, advancing across open ground single-handedly.

The next day, he rallied his section to engage and destroy two Mark Four Panzer tanks, one of which he personally put out of action.

In a subsequent action at Monte Cassino, Italy, he rallied his company after a German breakthrough and counter-attacked to break the German lines, bombing gun emplacements and holding the position till nightfall.

Sergeant Moran was captured and escaped, finding refuge in an Italian mountain village. When the village was attacked by a section of SS troops, he destroyed the troops and their weapons-carrier with a rifle and grenade attack.

His conduct, at all times, exemplified the fighting spirit of the New Zealand soldier.

THE LITTLE PUB near us isn't too bad; shadowy, the sharp stink of beer, the walls yellowed with smoke. Old-timers hunch over their pink racing forms. The barman, in shirt-sleeves and apron, is propped against his pumps like he's dead. There are a few younger blokes, ex-servicemen like me. 'Returned men' they call us now and chuck the women out of their wartime jobs so the 'returned men' can take over.

Our skills are no good in peacetime: stripping a machine-gun, laying a minefield grid, sighting a mortar, planning a night-raid. Being good at war counts for sod-all now.

Bates is sitting beside me, his artificial leg out stiffly. Gangrene had set in by the time they got him to an aid station. So the scouts are a memory now. 'Not fair on active lads, is it?' he was told.

Neither of us are drinkers, still nursing our first glass. I'm seriously annoyed with Bates. 'Did you have to shout the odds about Monte Bianco? I didn't want the flippin' VC.'

'Moran, you're the bloody limit. You've lived up to your dad and more.'

'You mean I've ended up just like him.'

'Had any job offers?'

I know that Bates is drifting. He wanted to be a physical-education teacher. I just shrug. Moran the VC winner's had a few offers. But I'm no prize cow for the highest bidder.

'Robbie, do you find it tough sleeping? Talking to people, making civilians understand —?' He breaks off. Real men don't get weepy.

'I just about never sleep. When I do, Mum says I yell the place down.'

They shipped some of us over to Britain for the awards. Mum in a new black coat and a hat with a big ostrich feather. Gaping up at the big crystal chandeliers in Buckingham Palace. The King pinning on my VC and saying King George the Fifth did the same for my father. That my father would be proud of me.

'Batesy, my dad's old CO, Rowlands, offered me a job in one of his department stores.'

'Jammy bugger.'

Rowlands did offer me a job. But we both knew I didn't fit behind a counter or a desk. Smart old coot, he suggested something a lot more in my line. 'There's a million rabbits down south. Good money for culling them. Also goats, deer, possums. Fancy it?'

'I'm on,' says Bates

Shooting. One army skill we can use. I hesitate, then tell him the rest. What Rowlands said about Amiens, 1918. Where Jacko rallied B Company and they fought to the last to stop Jerry. 'Hun' was the term Rowlands used.

'Well, old man Creel turned yellow and tried to bolt. And my old man shot him.'

'You're joking.'

'My old man plugged him in the arse with a bullet. Everyone knew, nobody did anything. Rowlands said I should know.'

Bates whistles and shakes his head. I wonder if young Richard Creel knew — maybe he suspected.

I want to stop thinking about Jacko's war, about

Creel, and about my war. As much as I can, because using a gun is all I'm good at. Stop thinking about those screaming SS men, and Mirella who wanted to —

'Who's flying, Robbie? Stop mumbling.'

'Nobody's flying, mate. Let's go south.'

'Slinger, are you sure about this car? It looks like a bomb to me.'

'Robbie, these Austins don't know how to quit. First-class engine, a little old lady owned this and only used it to drive to church on Sundays.'

'How come the dents then?'

'I never said she was a good driver. Listen Robbie, we're mates, just about blood-brothers. I'll knock ten quid off the asking price, can't say fairer.'

'Twenty quid more like it.'

'Twenty? Cripes, Robbie, I won't make a penny on the deal. But you're a mate. Fifteen?'

'All right. It'll get me down south?'

'My word on it, Robbie. Never let it be said I let down a mate.'

'If it doesn't, I'll be back.'

'Always welcome, Robbie, always welcome.'

Dear Robbie,

Not sure if I should write this, but I must. Read about your VC so am sending this c/o Defence Ministry, in hope it reaches you.

I am so sorry for Egypt. Tried to write but I think they got my letters. If you wrote, they got yours too. My bloody brother and my bloody mother.

I'm married, poppet, moment of madness. He's Indian Army Staff, awfully nice. We've had one sprog, another on the way. Heir and spare, you know. I think about you, Robert, and I do miss you.

Do be happy. Don't be haunted by ghosts, don't let a few years of war ruin the good years of peace. I read the citation, you were looking for death on that mountainside.

Do live, Robert. The time we spent together will mean something then. Lots and lots of love, do please be happy.
Your awful Pommy sheila,
Elly.

Dear Father Tommaso

You do not know me of course but I am Mrs Robert Moran and Robbie Moran, who stayed at your village, is my son. I am having this letter written in Italian by one of the Fathers in the Cathedral, so you will know what I am saying.

Robbie has that photo of Mirella and Teresa and looks at it a lot. He said your young men had asked about coming to New Zealand. Well, to be quite honest, I wonder if Teresa would come too, because I think Robbie would like that. He mentions her a bit.

He is very unhappy. He screams in his sleep and had a good job in the south but his car broke down and he was very rude about the man who sold it to him. He went with a friend who has married a farmer's daughter down there, so Robbie is alone.

I had a very nice visit from a Captain Rowlands who knew my husband, Jacko, in the last war. He says he can arrange something, so do think about it and I look forward to hearing from you.

Yours very sincerely,

Alice Moran.

The Hon. Rupert Creel

Dear Rupert,

Our first communication in some twenty-eight years. Our paths never did cross, never saw you at the reunions. Now Robbie Moran has the VC like his dad. Remember Amiens, where Jacko got the VC? Where you stopped that bullet in your backside?

I don't want the boy to end up like his dad. I'm sure you don't either. His mum says he has an attachment to an Italian family in that mountain village. Well, the girls and boys want to emigrate and that's why I'm writing.

You can smooth things over, make it easy. You're good at dodging around corners, so dodge around this one. Robbie's VC has brought up Amiens and Jacko again. The _Otago Daily Times_ is asking for my story but who wants to rake up old history? None of us, I'm sure.

Election coming up, so expect the usual donation. After I have heard from you, of course.
All the best,
J. Rowlands. Late Captain, Wellington Battalion.

Webley service revolver

Korea, 1951

No Siberian blizzards for once and no stinking heat. A warm spring day and very light breeze. Opposite our camp, a farmer is planting green rice shoots and treading with care. There are unexploded mines and shells in his field but he has a family to feed.

A little wide-eyed huddle of kids watches us. They will grab whatever we leave. Shank tosses them a candy bar and they fight over it silently. We're pulling out today; they'll have to find other rubbish-tins to scavenge.

I'm writing to Teresa, asking to make up. Maybe I'm not a bad husband like old Jacko, but an absent one. She was just too like Mirella and the nightmares would not stop. Rejoining the army for Korea was just an excuse — no matter what the papers made of it. I think I have it sussed now.

I will stay in the Army. Both of us, me and Jacko, were young men good at war and no good at peace. I'm better off in uniform among blokes who understand. Civvy life kills some soldiers, sure as a bullet.

Shank, who never thinks past the next mess-call, is still throwing candy bars to the kids. They're jumping so high that he cracks they should be in a lineout. I grab the box and chuck the whole lot over. That's worse, now it's a scrum.

So Teresa will be an army wife. Maybe I'll be a better husband. Get another glimpse of the God I saw at Monte Cassino. Faith and something to believe in. And try not to let my kids grow up scared of me. Hell, that's a bigger fight than Alamein.

The wind changes and a distant mutter of shellfire comes.

I'm used to that. I'll be hearing it all my life.

lothian Fiction

Antarctica's Frozen Chosen, Hazel Edwards

Beyond the Green Door, Kristan Julius

Blue Girl, Yella Fella, Bernie Monagle

Blue Murder, Ken Catran

Borderland, Rosanne Hawke

Carrie's Song, Bronwyn Blake

Chenxi and the Foreigner, Sally Rippin

Cupid & Co, Carol Jones

Dancing on Knives, Jenny Pausacker

Dear Venny, Dear Saffron, Gary Crew & Libby Hathorn

The Devil's Own, Deborah Lisson

Dreamcatcher, Jen McVeity

An Earful of Static, Archimede Fusillo

Edward Britton, Gary Crew & Philip Neilsen

The Eight Lives of Stullie the Great, Jim Schembri

Falling into Place, Kal Pittaway

Fat Boy Saves World, Ian Bone

Find Me a River, Bronwyn Blake

The Fourth Test, John Drake

Frames, Dorothy Simmons

Golden Prince, Ken Catran

Gothic Hospital, Gary Crew

Green Mantle, Gail Merritt

Heroes, Margaret Watts

Hot Hits, Bernie Monagle

Hot Hits — The Remix, Bernie Monagle

The Inheritance, Jo McGahey

Jacko Moran — Sniper, Ken Catran

Julia, My Sister, Bronwyn Blake

Katie Raven's Fire, Wendy Catran

Killer McKenzie, Eve Martyn

A Kiss in Every Wave, Rosanne Hawke
Leopard Skin, Sally Rippin
Lifeboat, Brian Ridden
The Losers' Club, Carol Jones
Mama's Babies, Gary Crew
Murder in Aisle 9, Jim Schembri
Not Raining Today, Wendy Catran
Operation Alpha Papa, D.J. Stutley
Operation Delta Bravo, D.J. Stutley
Operation Foxtrot Five, D.J. Stutley
Our Lady of Apollo Bay, Janine Burke
Poison under Their Lips, Mark Svendsen
Portal Bandits, Jim Schembri
The Rats of Wolfe Island, Alan Horsfield
Red Hugh, Deborah Lisson
Return to Warrah, Jo McGahey
Ridge, Dorothy Simmons
Riding the Blues, Jeri Kroll
Robert Moran — Private, Ken Catran
Rock Dancer, Bronwyn Blake
Settling Storms, Charlotte Calder
Shadow across the Sun, Margaret Campbell
Silver Mantle, Gail Merritt
Snigger James on Grey, Mark Svendsen
So Much to Tell You, John Marsden
Stalker, Hazel Edwards
Stitches in Time, Julie Ireland
Stuff They Don't Teach You at School, Josie Montano
Suburban Aliens, Nick Carvan
The Swap, Wendy Catran
Sweet Tea, Brian Ridden
Talking to Blue, Ken Catran
Time Out, Dorothy Simmons

Tin Soldiers, Ian Bone
Tomorrow the Dark, Ken Catran
Video Zone, Dorothy Simmons
Volcano Boy, Libby Hathorn
Voyage with Jason, Ken Catran
Watershed, Kathryn Knight
Welcome to Minute Sixteen, Jim Schembri
Whistle Man, Brian Ridden
White Lies, J.C. Burke
Wogaluccis, Josie Montano
Zenna Dare, Rosanne Hawke